US PEOPLE

MAXWELL GRUBER

Clovercroft Publishing

Us People

Published by Clovercroft Publishing, Franklin, Tennessee

Edited by Robert Irvin

Cover and Interior Design by Suzanne Lawing

Printed in the United States of America

978-1-945507-61-8

To My Parents
Thank you for believing in me

CONTENTS

ONE

STREET ODYSSEY

Call me Samuel. Actually, no, call me Sam. No one has called me Samuel since my days . . . well, my days back home. And Cam is always one to remind me of that when we are walking from shelter to shelter. Those are the worst kinds of walks. Sometimes, they're cold, sometimes they're hot, sometimes I feel like my legs are going to collapse under the weight of my backpack.

Sometimes I can hear people talking from their cars: "Is that a kid?" Sometimes I feel ashamed, sometimes I feel dismayed, and sometimes I feel lost. But sometimes I can feel the sun's rays massaging my face. The cars driving by fade out, the other "people" around me whisk away into the darkness, and the loneliness and feeling of being alone welcome me back. It's eerie and depressing, but for some reason it seems this has always been my home. A place to call my own, a shelter of refuge, a safe haven . . .

"Sam! Will you please hurry up?" It's Cam, shrilling to me in a deep, bellowing voice. "We're going to miss lunch at the shelter if you don't hurry your butt up." He is a few steps ahead of me. Each step I take forward—at a leisurely pace, I might add—Cam looks back in disgust.

"Just hurry!" he screams at me.

"Yeah, yeah. I'm coming! Maybe I could go faster if you didn't put so much shit in my pack! I feel like I am carrying enough for the both of us." I let out a large exhale through my nose as I angrily lug the overweight pack with each lumbering step.

"Hey! Hey!" Cam yells back at me. "What did I tell you about cussing! Just because 'they' do it doesn't mean you have to do it!"

Cam is being mean. Not just regular mean. I mean aggressive mean as he faces the reality he might miss the Salisbury steak and mashed potatoes that are served every damn Wednesday at the East Hills Shelter. A person might think that after eating Salisbury steak for the thousandth week in a row, one might get tired of it—but no! The look that Cam gets on his face when he is handed that beige tray with stale Salisbury steak and powdered mashed potatoes is enough to make you think it actually tasted good. Almost like it could be featured on some cooking show. The way Cam looks at that damn fake steak and mashed potatoes is how a girl would want a guy to look at her when he proposes. For him, it is an immaculate delicacy of the highest quality.

"Ugh," I sigh as I start to pick up the pace. "Cam, this pack weighs in the magnitude of tons! Can we stop for one moment, please?"

No reply.

We have to walk all the way across town from the West Valley Shelter to the East Hills Shelter. It's on the opposite frickin' side of town! We have been walking all through the morning. Occasionally running into the other "people" who were walking through town. Although I was fairly new to this setting—let's say eight months or so—the "people" were keeping an eye on me and making sure I wasn't getting into any trouble.

The worst of these is Cam. Not worst in the sense that he hates me or wants me to get hurt. In fact, it is the opposite. Cam is so protective of me that he makes me go with him everywhere I want to go and everywhere he wants to go. He is protective to the point that he will check my food to make sure I'm getting the proper nutrients and minerals necessary for what he calls "a growing boy." But I hate it when he calls me a boy. I am not a stupid boy; I am a man.

We continue walking under the heat of the sun. Today is a day when the sun doesn't feel pleasurable at all. It feels morbid and hateful. Like it is punishing us for trying to go get food on the other side of town. It's not like we don't have enough things to compete with already.

"This sucks! I can feel the sweat running down the side of my T-shirt, Cam! And again, this backpack. It feels like it is going to shatter my back."

Cam looks back with sheer disgust, but also with a shadowed look of worry. "I don't care if you have to drag it on the ground, we're going to get to the shelter on time. We're going to get Salisbury steak. And we're going to get there whether I have to drag you and the pack on the ground or not."

I roll my eyes.

"If you roll your eyes at me again, I am going to eat your food too, and then what're you going to do tonight when you're starving?" Cam sneers.

"You know I could always just go ask the volunteers for more. They are always happy to give a 'growing boy' like me more!" I sarcastically answer.

"Don't be a smart, Sam. No one likes a smart ass." Cam smirks back.

We continue walking through the heat of the morning and finally reach the halfway point between the east and west sectors of the city. The halfway point is marked by the I-74 highway that cuts the town in half, running north to south. It's commonly known as The Split. Normally, this is where we return at night if we can't get a bed at either of the shelters.

"Hey Cam! Can we rest ahead at The Split? I need a break!" I pause and heave. "Also, we have enough time. If we take a ten-minute break, we'll still be able to get to the shelter in time for your precious Salisbury steak." It's my turn to tease him as I motion my fingers in quotation marks.

Cam digs through his pants and pulls out a worn, rusted flip cell phone. He takes his other hand out of his pocket and rubs his thumb against the screen trying to read the time underneath all the lint and dust.

"Ten thirty-seven," Cam reports. "It will probably take us another hour to get to the East Hills shelter at a fast pace. The line begins to form at eleven-forty, so if you stop whining about the pack and hustle, we might be able to stop!" Finally, he lets out a small smile.

I want to look stern and deserving of this break, but I let out my own brief smile. We continue walking until we are underneath The Split. We call it The Split because the two lanes of the highway are raised from the ground, about two stories high, and the middle of the highway has a slight split between the opposing direction of roads. It's actually gorgeous. One can look up above and almost see the hum of vibration from the cars. It creates a sense of serenity as a person looks up into the sky.

We walk under The Split and locate the closest bench. My legs are ready to fall off at the hinges. I frantically look all around the area. I shriek when I see my favorite bench without anyone on it. I drop my pack and dart toward it. My legs no longer hurt and everything feels great as I speedily make my way toward my bench.

"Sam! Get back here!" screams Cam.

I ignore him. The wind pushes against my face as I press forward.

"Boy! Get back here!" Cam howls.

I freeze in place and feel my face flush. I slowly turn around and look back to see Cam all pissed and red.

"I told you not to call me boy anymore!" I scream. "No one can say those words to me anymore! I told you that!"

Cam doesn't falter. He's still pissed. "You lose your pack for a second and you're going to die out here. You lose your pack and you might freeze. You lose your pack and you might not be able to fend off the druggie with a knife. You lose your pack when I am not around and you are finished!" He is screaming right back at me.

"I told you to never say those words to me—ever!" I scream back. "You think I was being dramatic! Well, I'm not! Don't ever say those words to me again or I'll carve you until there is nothing left!"

A road runs perpendicular to The Split underneath and across from the benches. People crossing from the east part of town to the west, and vice versa, usually travel under The Split. At the moment, cars are lining up at the stoplight to exit The Split.

"Why is that man screaming?" A little girl's voice is ringing off in the distance.

"God, I hate driving through this homeless-infested stoplight!" rings out another voice.

My face is beaming red. The blood pulsates on the underside of my neck and vibrates the interior of my mouth. I am pissed. I hate those words. My eyes lock on Cam. He still has the same resolve. The stoplight turns green and cars begin to move slowly forward. Cam continues to stare at me. "Get over here and pick up your bag!" he screams.

I remain frozen and continue to stare angrily at Cam.

"Don't make me say it again, Sam!"

"Say it one more time. I dare you!" I am both cool about it and screaming at the same time, if that is possible.

Cam shrugs his shoulders and begins to open his mouth. I dig into my pocket and grab a makeshift shiv. It was made from a piece of jagged metal I found on the west side down by the river. I had taped one end of it and used some spray paint someone left in an alley to make it look like my own. Everyone has a weapon, and I wanted mine to be personalized.

I point the knife in Cam's direction. He stares back in silence.

The stoplight has turned from red to green and people in their cars remain fixed at the light—entertained by the spectacle before them. Car windows fall slowly as people place their elbows on the window and hold their phones upright—probably to take a video.

"Sam, don't do something you'll regret!" Cam shrieks.

A man in a black Jaguar now pulls up to the light and rolls down his window. A large, heavier man partially leans out the window and wheezes at the act of lifting himself.

"Boy, whatever you are about to go do, you better knock it off or I am going to call the cops," the man issues.

Cam turns his head back in my direction. "You hear that, Sam? If you don't knock it off, that man is going to call the cops. Then we will both be out of luck tonight and you are going to go back to that boarding school you hated so much. So, you tell me. What are you going to do? Try to stab me? Or are you going to put the knife away and we can both go get some Salisbury steak?"

I look at all the people waiting at the stoplight. All of them look scared and confused—because of me. There is a little girl sitting in the back of a silver Subaru Outback who is crying hysterically as she stares back at me. The light has turned back to red and all the cars are holding the same positions. Cars begin stacking up at the light and horns screech in the distance. People farther back, who have no idea what is occurring, scream profanities at the drivers in front of them.

I take a deep breath and look down at the knife. My hand hurts. I've been gripping the shiv so hard that the tape hadn't offered enough protection for my hand and blood is starting to run down. I loosen my grip on the shiv and place it back in my coat pocket. I lower my head and begin to walk toward Cam. As I get closer, the look on Cam's face changes from anger to one of dismay. I grab the bag and try to heave it onto my back. I buckle the straps and look up again at Cam. He always looked taller when he was mad. Six-foot-four always looks more like six-eight in those moments. I turn my head to see the people return their attention to the light and drive on. Cam pulls the flip phone back out of his pocket.

"Do you know what time it is?" Now he says it quietly, in a steady tone, with just an inflection of anger.

I look back up at him and slowly shake my head.

"Eleven-oh-seven. Do you know what that means?" It is now as though he is stating facts—quietly, angrily.

I raise my shoulders in a curious fashion and raise my eyebrows. "No, but I am sure you are going to tell me."

"It is currently eleven-oh-seven. It is going to take us an hour to get to the East Hills Shelter. The line begins at eleven-forty. We will not get there until twelve-oh-seven. Can you tell me what this means now?" Now the volume of Cam's voice is raising with each word.

"Umm. We're going to be late to lunch?" I say it mildly, as though I am confused.

"No shit, Sherlock! So now we're going to have to pick up the pace so I can get in line at the right time. If I don't get my Salisbury steak . . . " Cam places his hands against each other and cracks his knuckles. "Ohh!" He lets out a large exhale. "You're going to wish the man in the Jaguar had called the cops, because you're going to die." Now Cam has a crazed and frantic look on his face.

I chuckle quietly, then look again at Cam . . . he is dead serious. A vein that splits his forehead into two sides—left and right—is pressed against the surface, brimming.

I bite my lip and stare at the ground.

"Say you're sorry, then let's go." He is sneering, and he is angry.

I stay focused on the ground and quietly say, "I'm sorry."

"You're *what*?" Cam says, angrily.

I looked back up at him and scream: "I'm sorry! Now can we just go?! I don't want to be here anymore!"

Cam turns his back to me and then hastily makes his way down the street. "Hurry up!" he yells once more.

I sigh and sprint after him. My back and legs are still killing me. I never got a chance to rest and was on my feet the entire time we were fighting. I lower my chin as I break into a strut and continue to walk.

TWO

WELCOME TO EAST HILLS

"Cam! Please slow down! I can't keep running! I haven't eaten since last night. My legs have no energy left in them!"

"It's your fault that we're going to be late! It's your fault that you pulled that knife! And it's going to be your fault if I don't get my freaking Salisbury steak! It's only a ten-minute run away anyway, so shut up and just toughen up," Cam screams over his shoulder. "Back in my days in the military, we would have to carry our hundred-pound pack for twenty miles! You have carried it for . . . what? Maybe five?"

Cam lets out a large laugh as he continues hustling down the sidewalk.

I feel like I am about to quit. For anyone who has ever experienced the sensation just before quitting, there is nothing else like it. Everything screams at you to stop: your heart, your body, your mind. All in concert. And that's how I feel right now. My legs are screaming at me. I can feel my back cracking under the weight of this pack, and my eyes are starting to go dreary from dehydration. But there is no way Cam is going to let me stop even to take a sip of water. But, *let's try anyway,* I tell myself. "Cam, please. Just one second to stop and take a sip of water!" I am gasping. "How are you running for so long anyway?! You're thirty years older than me!" I'm fascinated by that—but also in anguish.

"Training for the war makes you strong. The pack that you keep screaming about is only one-fourth the weight I had to carry in boot camp," he yells back.

I keep forgetting that Cam has served in the war. Not just any war—the same war that that old asshole had served in. Except Cam came back with his sanity in check—or at least that's how it looked from the outside. I lift my head from sulking and peer ahead at Cam. He is still maintaining his speed!

"What time is it?" I shout, trying to lift my voice well ahead of me.

He reaches his hand into his jagged, vibrating pocket as he keeps running and pulls out the rusty flip phone.

"Eleven-thirty-seven!"

Thank god, we might make it on time, I think to myself. We aren't far now; just past the Myrtle building is the shelter. It's weird how everything changes past the Myrtle building. Lush, mirror-laden buildings that show the reflection of the sky dropping off into the commons and apartment complexes. The East Hills Shelter sits between two apartment complexes composed of brick and steel. Everything around here looks dirty, dreary. A dichotomy between the rich and poor, the subjugated and the wealthy. The buildings are a dreary gray, the streets are black and filled to the sides with gutters and trash, and even the sky looks as though a solitary cloud looms over the commons.

We slow the pace and now start to walk. "Thank god!" I scream as we slow to a leisurely pace. "I am a nineteen-year-old boy. I don't need to be running five miles across town every morning!" The shelter is a staggering five hundred feet away. Any farther and surgery would be needed to give me new legs.

My lungs feel like they are going to explode. Each inhalation is hot and heavy, while every exhale feels forced and painful. A torrential downpour of sweat runs down the sides of my body. With each passing second, what feels like the equivalent of a liter of sweat drips off my hair and into my eyes. Each salty injection of sweat feels like another reason to pass out on the sidewalk.

"Oh, crap!" I screech.

"I don't care if your leg just fell off. We ain't slowing down!" Cam screams.

Sweat has dropped into my eyes, and they feel like they are on fire. It feels like liquid salt and fire. My eyes are burning, and I need to wash them out.

"Just wait in line! I'll catch up with you in a minute. My eyes are killing me!" I yell ahead at Cam.

"Sam . . . " Cam responds, now in a tone of despair.

"Just go!" I say as I peer forward in a haze of blurriness and pain.

Cam looks back for a second and then looks forward. This happens three or four times before he finally just shrugs. "You better not be too long," he says, turning his head and continuing to walk toward the shelter. "Hey, and if it comes to it, I will be happy to eat your Salisbury steak on my behalf."

I make out the faint glimmer of a smile as Cam turns his back and hastily makes his way toward the shelter.

My knees feel contracted and weak. My eyes are still burning, only adding to the problem. No amount of rubbing, in any amount, helps. In fact, the more I touch them, the more dirt I can feel get into the socket. With each watery blink, the grime from my hands presses itself further under my eye and tugs at the sensitive skin. While holding my eyes shut, I lower my pack to the ground and feel around, blind, for the opening straps. Tears escape my eyes as I fumble for the straps. "Ahh, there they are," I say in disgust. "There's so much shit in here!"

With each passing moment, the pain becomes more intense. Why is this hurting so bad? It's just stupid sweat! I claw through the pack while my hands stumble around various obstacles. "No, that's my busted water bottle! . . . No, that's the plastic water bottle of whiskey! . . . No, those are my extra clothes. . . . No, those are binoculars." The desperation in my voice rises with each passing item. "Ahh, finally! The water bottle that isn't broken." With all the strength left in my arms, I rip the bottle from the backpack, heaving it upward through a myriad of garbage and excess clothing.

I rip off the top and vault the water bottle above my forehead. Without so much as a second passing, I invert the water bottle and smile as I stare upward into the stream. *I kinda feel like a stripper taking a water bath,* I think, chuckling softly. With each gush of water, I feel my eyes being cleansed and the salinity restored. "So much for rationing. Cam's going to be pissed, but what the hell? There's free water at the shelter."

I keep my eyes open the whole time the water splashes against the surface. The last bit of water drops into my eyes as I blink rapidly, several times. "Ow! Why do my eyes still hurt so much!" I scream.

"Hey! What's wrong, little man? Life got you down?" It's a voice coming up from behind me.

I turn my head and squint my water-filled eyes to see Mr. P and Crazy Bill walking along the curb.

"Looks like he been crying," says Crazy Bill as he chuckles and the wind wraps itself around his one solitary tooth. "I didn't know men were supposed to cry." He chuckles again—then coughs heavily into his jacket.

"I ain't been crying," I answer. "I've just been running so hard to this stupid shelter that I had sweat drip into my eyes and now I can't get it out." I am sobbing as I spill back my response.

Mr. P laughs, even bellows, as he rubs the underside of his belly. "Well, let me see if I can help you out!"

He turns to Crazy Bill. "Bill, I know you got all kinds of goodies in that shopping cart you're pushing around. Anyway, you got some hand sanitizer?"

Bill shudders for a second, then shakes his head violently. "Maybe I do, but I ain't sharing it. This here is my treasure and ain't nobody touching it, even you. Especially not the crying baby," Bill says, pointing at me. I'm now sitting helplessly on the ground.

"Dick," I mutter under my breath.

"What's that, boy? You got something to say to me?" Crazy Bill cocks his eyes and peers at me with his one good eye.

"Nothing, nothing," I say, sneering back.

"Well, that's too bad," Mr. P says. "If I had some hand sanitizer I'd be able to fix you right on up!"

I look toward my pack, still slouched on the ground with various items lying next to it. "I might actually have some," I say as I dig my hand into the main compartment. I search around—by feel only—for a couple of seconds, my eyes still pulsing with pain. "Here it is! Lucky. It was one of the items on top instead of the water bottle I was looking for earlier that buried itself on the underside of the pack!" I pull the small bottle out of the sack and look down. "High School Musical," the sanitizer reads. "Shit," I exclaim as I toss it to Mr. P.

He catches it with both hands and looks down at the bottle. He lets out a small chuckle and then gives Crazy Bill a look. Bill sneers and then looks back at me. "I didn't know you were some dancer!"

"I ain't! I found it on the ground a couple weeks back on the west side and figured I might need it!"

Crazy Bill chuckles as his bad eye wiggles up and down with no sense of direction. "Sounds like something some sort of dancer would say!"

Mr. P laughs, but finally lets out a big sigh and walks over to me. My eyes are still watering and, the more I open them, the more it feels like I want to scream. Each time my eyelid closes over my eye, a strong pulse emanates from the back of my eye socket.

"Maybe he's got the clap," says Bill as he keeps laughing, now harder. "I hear the clap makes all parts of your body hurt for no reason whatsoever."

Mr. P laughs, but then directs his attention toward me. "Alright, big man. This may hurt a little bit, but you gotta be strong and not scream or else Crazy Bill might trigger his PTSD." There is something about the way Mr. P talks. It makes a person want to be calm and collected. The peaks and valleys in his voice are something like that of a radio DJ or announcer. Each word is carefully enunciated, each sound humming in perfect pitch.

I look back at Crazy Bill. He is hunched over his shopping cart full of trash. A tire rim is sticking out jagged from the top, and his arms are lurched over it, something like a T-Rex. Every ten seconds or so, Bill's neck and the right side of his mouth twitch to the side. His head partially turns and his lips open.

"What's wrong with Bill?" I ask Mr. P.

"Well, Bill here has had a rough going of it, and people don't take the time to understand him like I do. Maybe one day if you're not being crazy and talking to yourself, I could come show you the ropes of how to make it big out here."

"Yeah. Talking to myself. Because I do that a lot," I murmur under my breath.

"See—that's what I mean." Mr. P laughs.

I look away from Bill as water streams down my face. I look back toward Mr. P and take a deep breath as he pops the top off the hand sanitizer bottle. I look up at him as he smiles. He squeezes the hand sanitizer into his hands.

"So, you just wanted the hand sanitizer to clean your hands?" I ask.

"A man should never eat with dirty hands, now should he?" Mr. P says, chuckling, as he takes a step toward the shelter.

"Wait, are you serious?" I yell.

"Nah. I'm just here joshing," he says, turning his head and smiling. The gold crowns on his two front teeth gleam against the sunlight. It is odd how, at that exact moment, the sun reflects perfectly from the Myrtle building onto them.

"Hold still," he says as he reopens the bottle of hand sanitizer and squirts the remainder onto his right index finger. "This may sting a little—well, a lot." He holds my eye open with his other hand and swipes the inside of it with the hand sanitizer.

I open my mouth to scream and Mr. P covers it quickly with his hand. "What did I tell you about screaming? It will set Bill off."

I can *physically* hear my eyes burning from the contact between my iris and the hand sanitizer. My eyes feel like they are going to burst—and that isn't even the worst part. The hand sanitizer makes my eyeballs feel like they are slimy and about to decompose. Each tear that works its way out of my closed eye slides out in an unnatural, almost alien, fashion.

"Feel better?" Mr. P is excited as he asks.

"No! It just hurts a fuck ton!"

I can hear Cam screaming inside my head, telling me not to swear, but this feels appropriate. It's not every day you have the feeling your eyeballs are about to decompose. Let alone wanting to scream—but someone won't let you, holding their hand over your mouth.

"Well, you'll feel better once you got some food in ya," Mr. P says as he places his hand on my shoulder and starts walking toward the shelter. Bill struts ahead, following him, then looks back and giggles. The sound of his broken cart scratching the concrete is deafening.

"Yeah, I don't think I need any more sensory dead spots for the day," I say, out loud, as I cover my ears with my hands and look up at the sky. The sky is still perfectly blue, all around the city, but for some reason there is one large cloud looming over the shelter. "So pretty," I say, sarcastically, as I push myself onto my feet. I grab the loose articles of clothing and other objects that had fallen out of my pack and stuff them back inside.

"One thing!" says Mr. P as he turns his body back toward me. "Wouldn't want you to ever stop dancing!" He chuckles in self-delight at his statement. Bill lets out a large, heavy, wheezing laugh while a symphony of sorts between the broken cart and the air rasping itself around his tooth works in concert.

I stand there, dazed by my eye and confused by Mr. P's comment. He tosses me the bottle in the air and I catch it and look down. I had forgotten about the logo.

I look up. With swiftness—and grace, I think—I lift my fist into the air and . . . point my middle finger.

Mr. P and Bill chuckle as they turn their heads. "Don't grow up too fast now, kid," Mr. P says, turning back to the shelter.

I bite my teeth and throw the bottle back inside my gargantuan pack. "He's never going to let that go now. Damn," I mutter. I throw the piece of fabric connected to the back of my bag over the giant compartment and latch it shut. I toss this seemingly immovable object back onto my shoulders and back and continue on toward the shelter.

Step by step, I trudge on. It's now just a mere fifty feet away. A line has formed outside the large glass doors. People seem on edge; there is pushing and shoving. A large security guard is facilitating placement in line by directing traffic. I look up and down the line outside the building.

"No Cam?" I ask aloud. "I'm sure he probably went inside."

I walk past the line and through the building's big glass doors. The building layout is simple. There's a front desk, meant to facilitate any-one who has questions or a problem, alongside the mail pickup. A large, looming white hallway extends itself to the back of the building, where a nurse and administrative offices are housed. Next to the hallway is a large metal staircase leading to the communal bathroom and showers on the upper floor. Finally, there is a common room/mess hall with grade school-style tables lifted down for lunch and dinnertime. On the north end of the room is a bar running parallel to the edges of the room that filters into giant metal openings, where volunteers gather to prepare and serve food.

I walk up to Judy, who is working the front desk today. "Hey, Judy! Have you seen Cam around? I was looking for him outside, but I can't seem to find him anywhere."

"Oh hey, sweetheart! My, looking awfully strong and big today! And I don't think I have seen anyone named Cam. What does he look like?"

I chuckle for a second and sigh. "There's no way you can miss him. Giant, behemoth, black man with military tattoos on his forearms and shoulders. Never lets me have any fun and made me run three miles today just so he could get the Salisbury steak and mashed potatoes."

She giggles to herself and turns back to one of the other volunteers working behind the desk. "Hey, LaTirra! Have you seen or heard of a man named Cam coming in today to grab food? Tall black man with tattoos."

The other volunteer turns her head slowly from her computer and peers back at Judy with disgust. "Judy! I am trying to make sure that everyone gets their mail delivered to them today. Unless this so-called Cam has got a package, then no, I haven't seen him today." LaTirra quickly turns back to her computer and then looks back to the man she was helping.

Judy turns back to me. "Sorry, sweetheart. We haven't seen him. Why don't you get some food in your stomach and then try looking for him? It might be easier when your stomach isn't empty."

I look down and place my hands underneath my shirt. My stomach growls just from being touched. I poke various points on it, and every sensation leads to a different sound—but basically it's an angry mob screaming to be fed.

"You're probably right," I sigh in response.

I turn away from the desk and head for the outside doors to get in line.

"Hey, big man! Why not come join us in line?"

I turn my head to see Mr. P and Crazy Bill waiting in line—about twenty people from the start of the food service.

"I don't want him waiting in line with us, P. I don't know how I feel about some dancer standing with us," Bill says, laughing, before breaking into a coughing fit.

Mr. P chuckles and smiled again. For some reason, the two caps on his front teeth look just as bright in here as they did outside against the sun. "I'm sure Big Sammy here won't take your food or steal from your cart. Besides, your cart is behind the front desk. I don't think Sam wants your stuff enough to distract the nice ladies at the desk and then sneak around and steal some valuable treasure." Mr. P looks back toward me, smiling. "Isn't that so, big man?" Mr. P gives me a wink.

Crazy Bill sneers for a second, twitches, then turns his back to me.

"I'll take that as a yes!" Mr. P says.

I sigh as I hop in line with them. Hundreds of people are now in line.

"Hey, no cutting!" screams a voice from behind me.

I move myself in front of Mr. P, out of sight of the people behind me. I look toward the people not waiting in line. The remainder of the folks who are too tired or too lazy to get in line and are either passed out on the floor or eating the residual bread from yesterday's dinner set out on a nearby rack. The large metal gates that block the common room from the kitchen crackle for a moment. A large metal-against-metal sound ushers into the room as the gates lift and expose the kitchen area.

The crew behind the counter is the same crew as every week. Mostly older men who are retired, a couple of priests, a couple of women who love to volunteer, and the workers from the shelter. Occasionally, one of the women will bring in her son, and he will man the dessert station at the end of the line.

I file through the line and reach one of the volunteers. She looks down on me and says, "Sweetheart, you look like a growing boy! How 'bout I sneak you a little something extra onto your plate?"

My face breaks into a smile. "Thanks, I appreciate it." As I turn away, my smile slowly descends, moving back to its more natural, neutral scowl. "It's not like I couldn't just come back and get seconds if I wanted more," I say in a whisper under my breath.

I get all the way through the line to the very end, where the straight conveyor-style service bends. I look toward the bend and, instead of the tall, beautiful blonde woman, there is a slender kid. He looks about two to three years younger than me—brown hair, pronounced complexion, large nose, very skinny. I sigh as I step forward; it is my turn for dessert.

"Hey man! You want some dessert? We got us a good one today!" This comes off as very eccentric. He cracks a smile and exposes his teeth. His front left tooth is larger than the right one, and dental staining is clearly visible on both teeth adjacent to the front teeth.

I peer down toward the dessert and then back up at him for a bit. The selection is a mixture of desserts donated by local bakeries: cupcakes, cake, little cookies, ambrosia—yuck—and some other foreign offering I can't make out.

I smile back at him and point to the cupcakes at the far end of the dessert tray. "Yeah, I'll take one of the cupcakes on the far back row."

The boy doesn't motion for the dessert at all. In fact, he just stares, almost stubbornly so, at my right arm.

I look down to where his eyes are directed. The scar ranging from the base of my hand up toward my forearm is bulging out from the rest of my skin. It glows slightly red under the cover of the halogen lights above. I reach for the shortened coat arm and rip it up over the exposed scar. I look up at the kid and scowl.

"Dang, that's a pretty gnarly scar. How did you . . . "

I can feel rage shoot up through my arms and into the base of my skull. I grit my teeth. I slam my hands onto the cart—sending all the plates of food slightly into the air. I reach up for the kid and grab him under the collar, pulling him forward. I stare into the kid's eyes; I can see the fear sinking in. His eyes dilate and the blood vessels surrounding his iris pulsate. I forcefully exhale.

"Hey boy! Get your hands off him!" A man shouts from behind the counter. I turn my head to see the volunteer workers all staring at me in disarray. The security service steps out from their office adjacent to the front desk and start walking toward me in a hurried fashion.

I look back at the kid. His arms tremble against my hands as they hold on tightly. I peer toward the giant commons room. The entire mess hall is staring at me. People behind me are getting aggravated from the holdup in line.

"Beat it, kid! We're starving!" a woman yells from over my shoulder.

"Stop making a scene! Sit down. I am starving!" screams another.

I look back toward the kid in a snarl and let go in one swift motion. The kid lets out a large, shuddered exhale and takes a big step back. His mom, who was about ten feet from him, motions for him to step toward her.

The kid's face is flush white. He swallows largely and the pit in his throat quickly moves up and down. And then . . . he begins sobbing—uncontrollably. Security walks up behind me. I turn toward them as they approach. Two gigantic men, one black and one white, with tattoos all down their forearms. Both cross their hands simultaneously. "We got a problem here, kid?" says the large white man.

I look past the two men and scan the whole floor. Everyone—men and women—have their hands holstered in their pockets. Everyone looks on edge, as if the smallest action, catalyst, or spark could set off a riot. The black security guard leans in closer toward me. "If you want to make an event, you are going to set everyone off. So, if I were you, I would take this food that has so nicely been given to you, and take a seat." He places his hand on my shoulder and squeezes. I wince from the pressure.

I turn my head back to the volunteers; all are just staring. Some look terrified, but some look on with total complacency. This is what we are to them . . . animals to be viewed. And this floor, this mess hall—this is our pit.

I look back at the security guard and nod. A weight lowers itself onto my opposite shoulder. "Come on, big man. Let's take a breather and go sit down for a second." A rhythmic and level voice rings out from behind me. I turn to see Mr. P smiling at the guards and trying to gesture me away. "He won't be any trouble; we will see to that." I look past Mr. P at Crazy Bill as he grimaces, then twitches, then goes back to grimacing.

I bite my lip and shrug his hand off my shoulder. "Just leave me alone," I mutter as I push my way between the two security guards.

I walk past the onlookers still staring in the large common room. Every table is taken—or people motion to me to keep walking. A corner, on the opposite side of the room, away from the masses, remains empty. I slowly trudge over; I can feel everyone's eyes hanging on me. I hurry to place my tray on the table and bury my head in my arms; I scream loudly into my hands. Next to the table are two men lying down, their eyes covered by T-shirts. One man lifts the shirt off his eyes to look around, slowly shrugs, and then places the shirt back over his eyes. I look out the window and can still see the looming cloud hanging over East Hills.

"Shitty weather, shitty food, shitty people," I whisper to myself as I stare out the window.

I feel a big hand place itself on my shoulder and I turn away from the window. It's Cam, who is grinning down at me with a large, illustrious smile.

"What do you want, Cam? Where the hell have you been? I could have used your help back in line." He moves to the other side of the table and takes a seat.

"Sorry, Sammy. I was so hungry and felt so weak when you were taking your sweet time outside that I ran inside to get in line before the line formed around the block." Cam heaves his large backpack onto the table and sighs. "It's been a long day so far, hasn't it?" He chuckles and then goes looking for something in his pack. "You need to be more careful around here," he lectures me.

"Why's that?" I demand, my tone aggravated.

"Let me point something out to you that I hope you remember." Cam points at the main pit as I turn my body in the direction of his finger. "Did you notice how when you caused a ruckus everyone became jumpy and holstered their hands in their pants and into their bags?"

I nod slightly and take a quick scan of the room. Most people are now minding their business, eating or playing a card game of some sort. Some are talking while others perform a myriad of other acts: talking to themselves, pacing back and forth, and more.

"You pull some stunt like that again and every person in here is going to have a field day. Everyone in here is armed, and I mean everyone. It may not look like it, but I can prove it to you."

"Oh yeah," I say, antagonizing. "Prove it!"

Cam sneers. "Do you see Old Lady Betty over there?"

I turn my head and locate Betty sitting at a table on the opposite side of the mess hall. Someone is talking to her, but something seems off. It almost looks as if she is daydreaming. She is paying no attention to the man talking to her; she frantically scans the room every five to ten seconds.

"It just looks like she is paranoid," I say as I turn my body back toward Cam.

"Look closer," Cam demands. I sigh and turn my body back in the direction of Betty—quite apathetically, I might add.

"I still see nothing, still."

Cam lets out a large, heavy sigh. "Do you notice how her left boot is pressed against the inside beam of the table strut?"

I look closer and even squint to more closely observe. "Yeah, but what about it? It just looks her leg is pressed against the table leg."

"Do you see how her left hand is dangling freely, but her right hand is occupied, flinching and toying with materials on the table?" Cam's voice becomes softer as the words fairly fall from his mouth.

"Yeah, but I still don't see what you are getting at. So she has her leg tucked in, what looks to me, a very uncomfortable position. So what?" *Make your point already*, I am thinking.

"Well, although she looks innocent, she isn't. Old Betty has mace and a shiv tucked away in her boot, and if you provoke her at all, she won't think twice about putting you down." He sighs for a second and then looks back at me. "For 'us people,' this is all we have. Take it away from some of them by causing a fight or being carried out and you will become a figurehead for their hatred. That means they will find you and hunt you down to restore balance. A weird sort of survival of the fittest with a morality bit. People don't like change, especially at the price of their well-being. So, next time you think of making a scene, consider the price of your actions." Cam relatches his backpack as he looks at me intently.

I take a deep swallow and give a quick scan of the room again. This time some things seem more evident. Some people quickly look toward me and sneer, while others plain stare at me to ensure I know they are watching. I feel a tingle go down my spine as I notice more and more people keeping tabs on me.

"It's not a good idea for us to stay here tonight, Sam," Cam says. He too is scanning the room.

I return my head to a normal position and then place it in my arms. I want to scream but don't want to bring any more unwanted attention to myself. "Wait." I quickly lift my head from my arms and look at Cam. "If we can't stay here tonight, then where are we going to go?"

"We're going to have to go back to The Split and find a place to sleep under the overpass, or somewhere around it," Cam says.

"Crap," I exclaim as I rebury my head in my hands. The only time I like sleeping at The Split is during winter. It's cold and people didn't linger long enough to screw with those who are sleeping.

Little by little, people slowly filter from the mess hall until there are only about fifteen people remaining. Lunch ended at 1 p.m., at which point the volunteers, security guards, and staff on duty open the doors and tell everyone to return at 6:30 if they want a bed to sleep in for the night.

"Sam, do me a favor and grab some of the excess bread from the rack so we have something to munch on later. I'm getting low on supplies," Cam says, checking his backpack one more time. "Actually, that's a lie. I *have no* supplies," he says, chuckling, though it's a sarcastic chuckle.

I nod in response and make my way for the bread rack. I pass the small chapel on the left where some people are praying. I round the corner for the bread rack and examine the rack up and down. Not much is left, maybe a quarter loaf of rye and what looks like some old, moldy honey wheat bread.

"Well, well, well. If it isn't the buttercup who caught my eye. We don't want no more scuffles here, boy. If you pull some shit like that again, then we're going to have a problem. But the *fun* kind of problem," some big guy is saying as he opens his mouth and exposes his rotten teeth.

He pulls me closer and smiles. His breath reeks of sulfur, cigarettes, rot, and some other indistinguishable smells. I look into his eyes. His pupils seem to cover the whole of the internal field of his iris.

"Sure thing . . . sir," I say as I grab at his hands and throw them off my shirt. Two men and a lady behind them sneer and chuckle for a few seconds. "Now run along, buttercup," the first man says. "We have a playdate later that you are not going to want to miss."

A chill shoots down my spine and my heart races. I look at the bread rack, panic, and reach for the first bag that comes into view.

"Don't forget this scuffle today, sweetheart," the man says as I walk away.

"Asshole," I say under my breath.

Cam is waiting for me at the table. I reach under the table, grab my pack, open the main compartment, toss the bread in, and seal everything up. I heave the heavy pack onto my back. I let out a heavy sigh of panic. Cam smiles, then giggles, as he watches me frantically gather my belongings. Although we had been eating for a significant amount of time and I sat during the entire meal, the pack still feels incredibly heavy. I feel as though my abdomen is going to cave in on itself—and all that will be left will be the backpack.

We walk to the doors and make our way outside. Passing through the doors on the way out, I look toward the sky and can still see the cloud sitting over East Hills. I look toward the surrounding city—blue skies. Not a single cloud in the sky today—except for the one looming directly over the shelter. There is still plenty of time in the day to make it back to The Split. I look toward Cam and smile briefly.

"Hey, Cam. You know what I want to do right now?" I say, enthusiastically.

"Yeah, what's that? Get into another fight with someone? You know what? We should start a fight club!" Cam chuckles at his thought as he bends to his side and coughs into the interior of his coat.

I look at Cam. "No, we're not going to start a fight club. Besides, you would get your ass whupped. I, on the other hand, would be champion."

Cam looks right back at me, one eyebrow raised. "I told you not to cuss! And . . . if you were or are the champion of this said 'fight club,' then there's no way it is an actual fight club."

I shoot Cam a look of scorn and he flashes a large, white smile. "Anyway, we are getting away from the point. What I want to do right now is try to make some money for tonight, since we definitely won't be coming back here."

"Well, if we aren't coming back here, why don't we walk toward the West River Shelter?" I ask.

Cam tries to keep a straight face, but the bottom part of his lip wiggles as he tries to contain a laugh.

I let out a heavy sigh and look Cam's way in disappointment.

"What, you don't want to walk ten miles back to the shelter?!" Cam busts into a laughing fit. And every time he surfaces for a breath of air, he immediately starts laughing again. "See . . . "—he is crying, tears literally swelling from his eyes. "It's funny because . . . " He takes a deep, large breath. "It's funny because there is no way you would ever want to do that!" Tears continue to stream as he continues to laugh.

Cam looks my way again. I lift my hand in front of his face. Cam looks on in wonder. I complete a simple act.

I flip him off.

THREE

THE SCHOOL OF PERSUASION

Making money was something that came easy for me. I was never sure if it was because I was young or if I seemed handsome to some people, but regardless of how much I tried, I always seemed to walk away with a decent sum of cash. Well, at least enough money to buy myself a solid meal, a nice drink, and still have enough to store something away in my pocket.

Cam, on the other hand, was a different story. We would travel to different spots so it didn't seem like we were competing for the same group of people. Wherever the spot, Cam almost always walked away with nothing. I could never tell if it was how big and intimidating he looked or whether he was just bad at getting money. But most of the time, he was living off me and my cash.

Most of the time, though, he would take whatever money I had remaining and place it in my account at National Bank for what he called "safe keeping."

* * * * *

30

We walk out the shelter doors; the sun is finally shining on us. "It's getting hotter," I say to Cam as he surveys the surroundings. Cam turns his head in my direction and smiles.

"That's a good thing," he says. "You're going to make more money. People feel more inclined to give when they feel pity for you, especially since you're just a kid."

"I'm not a kid," I yip back at him. "I am nineteen. I am pretty sure they stop calling you a kid at around fourteen."

Cam grins back—both his eyes closed. "You are still a little princess to me," he says, laughing and rubbing his belly.

"Well, you may be right. A little sweat and some acting may generate some more money," I say. I look again at the sky. The sun is beaming down around the clouds in an almost concentric fashion.

"Hey, Cam. What time is it right now?" I ask as I watch people filter out of the shelter heading in different directions.

Cam looks up at the sun and then down at his shadow. "Not a damn idea. Maybe one-fifteen?"

"Can't you just check your phone really quick?"

"Nah. The phone died while we were inside the shelter and I wasn't able to find a power jack to plug it in."

"Shit." That's all I have in response.

Cam turns his head back to me and looks disappointed. He is just about to open his mouth when I interject.

"I know, I know. I won't swear. Sorry. Sorry." I motion my head down, like a puppy, like I seem disappointed in myself. I stare at the ground for a second, then look back at Cam.

"What corner do you want to take today? Even though it doesn't matter. Because I am going to make all the money."

I can make out a smile playing on the corners of Cam's face. He shakes his head and laughs. "I don't know, Sam. Today feels like the day to me. The day for something special to happen. Like today, I feel like I am going to make upwards of a hundred dollars." Cam rubs his fingers together and then flicks the imaginary dollars into the air as if he was living it up in a strip club. "Oh, I am going to be rolling in it. You watch. You will be jealous."

I laugh for a second and then look both ways down the road. "Since my pack is so heavy, why don't I take the intersection for the off ramp of I-3, since it's closer, and you can take Main Street, downtown?"

He thinks for a second and then gestures in agreement. I turn my body, heading east, and begin walking toward the I-3 off-ramp.

"Sam, be careful! I'll meet ya at The Split later tonight for dinner. We'll see which one of us can take the other out for eats!"

I turn my head back to see Cam grinning as he rubs his fingers together and starts humming.

I turn back in the direction of the Myrtle building and set out. I walk through the downtown financial district, watching as my reflection bounces from one perfectly cleaned glass building to another. After about twenty minutes, I finally arrive at the I-3 off-ramp out-point. I look up; it may be about 2 o'clock, but I have no idea. Cam's the one with the phone. I look around briefly to see if anyone else has set up shop—and even if someone has, the spit-out is arranged in such a way that multiple people can work the street at the same time.

The layout is interesting, perfect for panhandling. Two roads converge into a single stoplight. The road arching downhill from the hospital, for those trying to reach downtown, flows into the left-hand side of the main arterial, while I-3 has an exit branch into the stoplight. The down-ramp from I-3 flows into the road on the right. A concrete median separates the two avenues, which converge into one after the stoplight. Two people can work the road at the same time if each one stays on their side. I had heard of Crazy Bill working the median—but that was just a rumor.

Again, I scan my surroundings and decide to set up shop on the left-hand side of the street. I figure people who are coming in on an artery are more likely to slow down, see me, and give money, versus those coming off the highway and trying to get downtown. Those people always seem to give less because they are in such a hurry.

I drop my pack on the ground, open the latches, and reach into my bag searching for my sign and blanket. All the excess stuff in my bag piles to the top. I feel around with my hands and graze against the softness of the blanket and the rough, hard edges of cardboard.

I look down at my sign with a gaze of satisfaction. It reads: "Too poor for plastic surgery, stuck here … until I can afford it. Post-surgery, please call." I listed the perfect number in hopes of people calling. The best part is the number I listed is the business number for the mayor's office! It always makes me smile to think about people randomly calling the number only to discover it's the mayor's office.

"Hey, big man! You mind if I work the other side of the road?" A voice calls out from across the cacophony of horns and street cars. Even with all the sounds echoing around in the street, I can still distinctly make out the bellowing voice of none other than Mr. P. It is almost as if the cars amplify the better parts of his voice.

I look up from my pack to see Mr. P jumping on the other side of the road trying to get my attention. I look back down at my bag for a second and then pause. I've heard the rumors about how good Mr. P is at working the streets, and I'm not sure if I want to share my haul with him today. *I need money for dinner.* Before I can make up my mind, though, Mr. P is running across the street to my side, nearly getting hit by a big black SUV while in stride. He chuckles as he spins to the side and waves the black SUV forward.

"Big man! Big Man! I have an idea. Instead of working separate sides of the streets, how about we work the street together and I can give you some tips? Maybe try and up your game a little for how you can be more successful." Mr. P stands directly in the sun as I look up in a squint. He is motioning me, with his hand, to say something—doing so repeatedly.

I've always wondered if the rumors are true. It's said in the shelter sometimes that Mr. P is so good he almost makes this look like a true profession. Like something he went and trained for. Almost as if he enrolled in a school of persuasion and walked away the top student. Something to provide for a family. Something to make others wonder why he is so good. "Yeah," I say in a diminished tone. "We can work on the same side of the street. But only if some of that magic of yours I hear about rubs off on me."

Mr. P giggles to himself as he turns his body in the direction of the cars and smiles. The gold crowns on his two front teeth gleam in the sun. The gleam shoots down off the contour of his face—almost, it seems to me, making him look divine.

"Sammy, you should know." He chuckles again. "It's not magic, it's human nature." He takes a step forward, then pauses for a second. He turns his head back to me and smiles. "You do know why they call me Mr. P., don't you?"

I shake my head.

"The P stands for persuasion." He lets out a deep, rhythmic laugh as he starts walking toward a row of cars. After a couple of steps, he pulls out a medium-sized cardboard sign from inside his coat.

The cars lined up at the stoplight wait patiently for the light to change. I look toward the cars. Almost every person is either peering down at their phone, sighing, or tapping their fingers, anxiously, against the top of their steering wheel. I look back toward Mr. P. He lets out a deep, heavy sigh, closes his eyes for a second, and then . . . shakes his body violently back and forth. "Hey everybody! Let me hear it! Let me see it! I'm just here to make your day better."

I sit up quickly and walk closer to the road. *He must have something ingenious written on his sign,* I tell myself confidently. I am thinking the sign reads: *All the money helps my addiction.* Or maybe: *Change isn't the only thing Obama intended.* I lean my head to the right to read the sign—and then stand there in shock.

SMILE!

And it's in big, black, bold letters. The rest of the cardboard is blank. Nothing covers the remainder of the space except for a single crease which, I'm guessing, is where he folds the thing. I look at the people lined up at the stoplight and something seems different from normal. All the people who had been busily doing various things—checking their phones, waiting anxiously, blasting music, fiddling with their CD players—are all now watching. I watch curiously as their eyes scan Mr. P as he jumps up and down and walks side to side. Every motion, every action—they are hooked. They are entertained. Curious.

I look closer. The disgusted looks of a few are washed away by the curiosity of most others. Mr. P walks up and down the street and points at individual people. If a person doesn't look back and smile, he begins jumping up and down and performing crazy feats. One by one, I watch as the dull expressions on people's faces change to looks of enjoyment and laughter. The whites of their teeth gleam against the sun. Everyone suddenly looks happy. I can feel *my body* loosen up and relax as I watch, my heart feeling warmer with each person laughing and smiling.

"Hey man! Over here! Let me help you out!" Mr. P's head whips around as he scans the road. A man is holding money outside his window. Mr. P runs over in a blazing fury, talks to the man a moment, then gives him a high five. The man laughs as the wrinkles on his forehead scrunch together in a tight bundle—and then relax.

One by one, I watch as people laugh, roll down their windows, and high five Mr. P. He chuckles giddily as people smile—genuinely—back at him. After a small conversation, they offer him money, then wave him off and roll up their windows. *This man is a savant. A true genius on the streets.* Every rumor about him . . . they were all true. People love him. He is doing something only he can do: persuade and promote. "Maybe this is what he meant by 'human nature,'" I say—out loud to myself—as I stare at the ground in reflection.

The sound of footsteps grows louder. Mr. P walks in front of me to a white compact Lexus and peers inside in disappointment. I lean to the side and can see a man inside staring ahead with a stern, flexed face. Mr. P walks right up to the door and knocks on his window. The man looks stunned. Through the reflection of the window, I can see Mr. P pointing to the sign and smiling, showing the man his big gold caps. The man in the car rolls down his window to create just a small slit.

"Get away from my car, Hobo. I just got this cleaned and I don't want your dirty germs or whatever disease you have seeping in."

I can feel a chill tether itself to my spine and work its way down, lifting each individual hair as it passes. I press my hands against the ground in fury. *How can someone be such a jackass? Mr. P isn't doing anything wrong.* As I push my hands into the ground, I look to see Mr. P . . . continuing to smile at the man. Mr. P takes a step back from the car and continues smiling. The gleam of his teeth radiates off the white paint and shimmers in all directions. And Mr. P is ready with a response.

"My apologies, sir! I just wanted to ensure that you have an amazing day and that you smile." Mr. P's voice is somewhat hushed, soothing—and he continues smiling.

"Just stay away from my car," the man says as he directs his attention forward, the small dimples between the muscles in his face becoming apparent.

Mr. P says nothing but does one thing: he lowers the cardboard sign from above his head to the man's eye level. The man does nothing; he merely continues staring forward. Seconds pass and nothing has changed—the man continues to stare forward. I look back toward the cars lined up behind the Lexus. Countless people look on in curiosity as Mr. P continues to smile.

I look back at the man in the car. He slowly turns toward Mr. P. The muscles in his face twitch up and down; it looks like he is trying to hold in a brief smile. "Come on man, you'll feel better!" The smile on Mr. P's face gets even bigger. I chuckle as I lower my body back toward the ground and feel the warmth working its way back into my body.

The man's face cracks a small, white smile.

"See! That's what I am talking about!" yells Mr. P, joyously, as he jumps up and down in excitement. "One little smile! That is all it takes for you to have a good day! Ya feel better now?"

The man's complexion shifts. A cold, unpleasing face before is now transformed into one of warmth and friendliness. The man lets out a deep chuckle. "You know what?" the man says, looking down briefly. "I do, I feel a lot better."

Mr. P smiles and backs away from the car. "I hope that smile carries you through the day and that your day is amazing!" Mr. P winks and turns his back to the car as he raises his sign forcefully up in the air. He waves it back and forth and yells enthusiastically at cars. I direct my attention back to the man in the Lexus. He frantically looks around his car, pivoting his head left to right, up and down. Finally, he rolls down his window—completely down.

"I don't have any cash on me, man. I'm really sorry." A quarter of the man's body is leaning out the window as he stares intently at Mr. P. "I am really sorry, man!"

Mr. P doesn't get mad; in fact, the expression on his face doesn't change at all. He turns his body back to the man with his continuing smile. "Your smile is all I needed today, man," he says. "You don't owe me anything. That will get me through the day." His words seem completely sincere; in this moment, there is no reason not to believe Mr. P.

The man chuckles as a small wave of red overtakes his face. "Well, I hope you have a good day, and I promise, I'll save some spare change for you tomorrow."

Mr. P now completely turns his body around, directly facing the man. "Much love, sir," he says as he slowly thumps his chest.

At this point, the driver behind the Lexus is on his horn, trying to get the man to pull forward. The light has changed and the driver of the Lexus has become so distracted by Mr. P that he hasn't even noticed. The man finally rolls up his window, waves, and drives forward.

I stand there in shock and awe. A flurry of emotions wells inside of me as I watch all eyes lock on me. Within moments of Mr. P taking the scene, all feeling of apathy and doldrums on this street has ceased. Joy and genuine laughter surge past along with distant honking horns and sirens. I stare forward at Mr. P in disbelief. Never have I heard a man promise one of us money with such intent, in the way this man has just promised Mr. P.

Mr. P sticks his sign back into his coat and zips part of it up as the cars behind him whip past. He lowers himself to the ground and lets out a shallow sigh. "All in day's work," he says with a light laugh.

He turns his head toward me with his eyes closed and simply . . . smiles.

The gold caps have never looked brighter.

I open my mouth as I stumble to find the words needed to express the myriad of feelings surging through my head. "H . . . h . . . how?"

Mr. P smiles, laughs. "When you see 'us people' getting up and trying to work the streets every day, what is something that you always notice?" he asks me.

I think to myself for a second before answering. "I guess that we all want the same thing. We all have these signs that say, 'Please help' and 'God bless' and other things like that. We all want money to do whatever we want with it."

"Exactly!" he exclaims as he looks back toward the stoplight.

It's still green. He peers back at me.

"I don't understand how you did that, though." I decide to persist in my questioning.

"Well, when you think about it, the concept behind it is fairly simple," Mr. P starts. "When 'us people' are asking for money, we are trying to illicit a feeling of pity and helplessness within the people who look at us. They see someone is hurt or needs help and it appeals to their altruistic nature—the aspect that makes them want to help others. What I am offering is simply a shift in thought. A shift within an economic aspect. I offer to do something for them, something that people often forget to do. Smile! Let those sad thoughts fade away for at least a single moment and let them enjoy something different and new. In doing so, I am offering these people a momentary service. I have given them something! Whether it is a moment of happiness or clarity, or anything else, they feel they have received something! And when people feel they have been given a gift, psychology dictates that they feel the need to return the favor. Right?"

I nod in astonishment as Mr. P continues breaking down his scheme.

"Don't get this confused! Returning the favor doesn't always mean money. It can mean a whole pile of things. A big smile, laughter, a promise, maybe a few bucks if they can spare it—anything will do! All that I am is a businessman. I offer something new, something they haven't seen before. I am offering them . . . innovation." Using his fingers for air quotes, he places this last word in quotation marks.

I am *still* having trouble picking my jaw off the ground. I am envious. This man has it all figured out. He is a legend on the streets, but seeing him work has been something else entirely. I have heard of people trying to replicate his act. Emulate the same sign. Smile just as bright as he does. But none of it was to any avail. *Mr. P is the only one who can do what he does,* I say to myself. The only one who can interact with people on this level. Make them truly feel like he is offering them something. The chance to smile. The chance to laugh. The chance to take the mundane out of their day, even if only for a few moments.

That . . . that is something I don't have, I am sure: the wow factor.

"You want to give it a shot?" Mr. P says, smiling, as he looks down on me sitting on my blanket.

The feelings and emotions of awe quickly turn to dismay and embarrassment; I dart my head toward the ground. "I don't know if I can do it as well as you. Umm, I am not the best in these situations."

Mr. P chuckles as he spreads his legs out on the concrete while simultaneously massaging his belly and picking out something from between his teeth. "Anybody can do it!" he proclaims. "You just need a little swagger. Just make sure that people smile! All you gotta do is be genuine and people will react in the same way. That is the most important aspect of this whole thing!" He spreads his hands in a bombastic manner and smiles once more. "Welcome to the playground, Sammy!"

I swallow—a huge one. I quiver as I can feel the saliva scraping against the insides of my throat and dropping to my stomach below. I swallow again.

"Alright. I'll give it a shot."

"My man!" chortles Mr. P, ecstatic. "You are going to need this!" He unzips part of his jacket, reaches in, and pulls out the medium-sized cardboard sign.

I swallow again and push myself up off the ground. I peer at the cars, now coming to a stop. My vision suddenly seems a little hazed. But here I am.

"Just be yourself, big man! If you need any help, I will be right here behind you." Somehow, Mr. P's words are comforting. He motions toward the cars now stopped. "You got this!"

I flip the sign around and freeze. I stare out at the sea of cars and panic. This is something totally new. Normally, I sit on a blanket on the nearest curb and stare at people with a solemn look of pity on my face. No, this is much different. Mr. P wants me to *engage*—to talk to other people. I swallow harshly once more and peer down at the sign. The large bold letters—*SMILE!* —gleam back at me. I lower the sign and stare back at Mr. P.

He just smiles at me and motions with a thumbs-up.

I close my eyes and swing the cardboard sign above my head—with all the force within me. I let out a quick exhale and open my eyes.

A sea of eyes are locked on me. A feeling of penetration. A feeling of being violated. All the whites—eyes, teeth, car color—reflect the sun as people look on at me with an array of emotions. I feel like an animal on display at the zoo—starring up at the faces of those who are yet unappeased.

"Smile, big man!" Mr. P says, his voice now quiet as he leans closer to me. "You can't just stand there with a blank face and not smile. That is the whole shtick."

I am trying to force myself to smile, to at least get *something* on my face. I look around at all the cars—and all I see are cold faces staring back at me.

"What a freak!" say two teenage girls driving a Jeep Wrangler in the second lane over. They giggle to themselves as the driver pulls her phone from her pocket and raises it vertically toward me.

"Oh, poor boy," says a woman driving in the lane closest to me, about three cars back.

"Get a job!" screams a man in the farthest lane. He is driving a big white truck with an American flag streaming down the right-hand side of the chassis.

A feeling of hollowness emanates from my stomach and spreads like wildfire through my body. First down through my legs, then it wraps around my torso and slithers its way up my spine into my neck. Individual stars populate my vision as I frantically look around the sea of gazing eyes. I look over at Mr. P, and he is staring at me, hoping for something amazing to happen.

"Come on, Sammy! Give 'em a big one! Don't just stand there!" Mr. P places his hands against the ground to push himself up.

My legs tingle against the faint pressure of a little wind. More stars are populating my field of view as I continue frantically scanning the roadway. The girls in the jeep continue laughing—both their phones are now directed at me.

"Fuck this!" I scream. I lower the sign to my eye level, stare at the large letters—*SMILE!*—and, with one quick heave, toss it into the first lane of traffic.

"Sammy, what the hell!" screams Mr. P.

I quickly spin toward my bag, close the latches on top, and rapidly swing it onto my back.

"Where are you going?"

I turn my head backward for a moment to see Mr. P standing in a slumped position, his hands pointed in the air.

"Anywhere but here!" I yell as I continue walking. I am no longer in the mood for working the streets. Food no longer sounds enticing. I just want to be gone—gone from this place. My face and arms pulse with waves of electricity as I frantically try to shake them free of the oscillations.

"I should have just done it my way. It would have been so much easier. I wouldn't feel like this now," I say in a heavy breath as I walk quickly from the panhandling spot. Normally, I sit there and people toss me a coin or a buck for being down on my luck.

I just can't get the image of the two girls out of my head.

"Screw those girls!" I yell to no one in particular.

"Where should I go?" I whisper to myself. I am utterly confused. I spin my head around, now two full blocks away from that place of humiliation. I turn back to see Mr. P, now a small spec, trying to pull his cardboard sign from the street.

"Cam! I can go see Cam!" I yell to myself. But I don't want to go to Cam's area and bug him while he was working. I also don't want to go to The Split and sit alone. And most of the other "residents" are probably passed out under the overpass from booze, drugs, or who-knows-what.

Screw it. I'll walk to the park. I can hunker down on a bench and at least get a decent rest. The sun is beaming down and, in the distance, forms small distortion patterns against the hot temperature of the pavement. I brush the beaded sweat off my face while rubbing the remaining part of my face with my coat arm.

Step by step, I make my way through the downtown financial district. A fugue state of discontent follows each step; I can't help but think about those girls. Each time I close my eyes, even just briefly, I see them laughing at me. Each time both lift their phones from their pockets and laugh maniacally. Each time a feeling of hollowness reemerges from the bottom of my stomach. Each time my legs feel weak and fatigued. I brush a bead of sweat from my face as I squint at the gleaming sun reflecting off the buildings.

"Honestly, how the hell could this day get any worse?" I am talking to myself. "First, that stupid fight with Cam. Then that stupid kid in line back at the shelter. Then those dumb broads in their stupid jeep."

I slap myself in the face with a stern and flexed hand. My face pulsates from the removal of my hand. "Just remember what Mom used to say when you are having a bad day!" I say to myself. "Just keep your head held up high and try to shake yourself loose from the bad day's grip." I say this over and over in my head.

The sun now is slowly covered by the only cloud in the sky. A dark, looming cloud that looks eerily like the one that covered the shelter earlier in the day. I exhale sharply as a shadow draws itself across my face.

Although the air is starting to cool, I can still feel the sweat dripping down my sides. "What I wouldn't give for a shower!" I scream. The people walking on the opposite side of the street stare at me. A man dressed in a red polo shirt holding hands with a beautiful blonde woman. Both stare at me in a distressed manner.

"Can I help you with something?" I scream. They both immediately bury their heads to their chests and speed-walk away.

My face still feels flush. All I want to do is sit down and look up at the partial blue-gray sky. I just want this day to be over. I want to be rid of this stupid nagging in the back of my head. I want to be back where I started, back at the beginning, back home in my bed with three years taken off the clock of my life.

I continue through the financial district and finally reach the park, located next to the waterfront. I sigh in relief. The closer I get to the waterfront, the less weight I feel my legs taking.

The waterfront layout is simple. It's a massive park with a large fountain in the middle. When it's hot out, such as today, kids ranging anywhere from three to fourteen will run through the fountain and try to avoid the spouts of water shooting up from the ground. If it's extremely hot, spouts will shoot water from the top of the water structure and soak the kids running underneath. Next to the fountain is a carousel with classical music playing in the background. A river, which runs behind the carousel, splits the north and south parts of towns. Although it is easily accessible from the waterfront, the river quickly drops off into a hydroelectric dam, which powers most, if not all, of the city.

I spot an empty bench in front of the fountain and walk over. I heave my bag off my back and hang my head to the ground. I am exhausted. Drops of sweat work their way down the wrinkles on my face and fall to the ground. I chuckle to myself—actually chuckle—as I continue staring at the ground. "You would think that after eight months of being out here on my own, I would be able to walk like fifty miles a day or something." I look to my side at the bulging backpack. "Maybe if I wasn't hauling around a huge sack of shit!"

I look up to see a couple of children running through the spouts, screaming. It looks fun. I can feel the muscles in my face relax as each child screams out in pure enjoyment. Their mother—or guardian, whichever—is screaming at them to come dry off because it's becoming cloudy and dark. One of the kids stops and just stares at me on the bench. I impulsively smile back. She's a little blonde girl wearing a pink one-piece swimsuit. I lift my hand and slowly wave at her in a genuine manner. She giggles, smiles, and turns her back to run to her mom.

I look at the ground and notice how ragged my shoes have become. The sole is starting to fall off my left shoe and my big toe can clearly be seen by anyone standing near me. "Damn, I need new shoes," I softly say to myself

I prop my bag against the side of the bench and lower my head onto it. At least all the shit in this bag is good for something—it acts as an excellent headrest. I let out a large exhale in a rare moment of contentment and then stare up at what is now a patch of blue sky. Clouds, now forming, loom around the open blue gap in an almost predatory manner.

"At least it's pretty," I say out loud as my eyes slowly flicker shut.

FOUR

LUCIDITY

I woke up from a deep sweat. The room around me was laced with the shadows of bushes swaying outside the window against the wind. It was hot. I could feel my clothes and the few sheets that were covering my body soaked in sweat.

"I would kill for a fan right now," I said as I brushed the sweat off my forehead and then wiped the rest of my face with my pillowcase. I removed my legs from underneath the bedsheet and looked to my side of the bed for the clock.

"Ugh. I thought it would be at least six-thirty," I said in disbelief at the clock, which reads: 3:32 AM.

I hoisted myself to the ground, looking for my shorts. I needed water. My head was killing me, probably from dehydration and sweating everything out that I had drank in the last week. I looked on the ground but couldn't see a thing. The outlining of light from the outside was only partially illuminating the room: its upper half. I felt around the floor with my feet.

"Damn. Where are my stupid shorts?" I whispered to myself, hoping for contact at any point. I continued to search with my toes, then turned my body toward the door—and that's when it hit me.

"Smoke?" I said in disbelief. "I smell smoke!"

I ran to the door and hit my knee hard against the edge of my desk. "Ow, shit!" I screamed. I ripped open the door to the hallway and was met by more darkness. The smell of smoke was now quite pungent. It was penetrating my nostrils and burrowing itself into my lungs. I covered my mouth and tried to feel my way down the hallway towards the stairs.

"Vrrrrr! Vrrrr! Vrrrr!"

The smoke alarm went off above me. It was deafening and there was nothing I could do to quell the sound destroying my ears. Between the smoke floating around and the loud screeching, I figured it would be better for me if I kept my hand over my mouth.

"Ahhh!"

A scream rang out from downstairs. I pressed my body against the edge of the hallway as I shimmied myself toward the flickering red light at the end of the hallway.

"Ahhh!" The scream was even louder than the alarm blaring in the background.

I squeezed my hands against my mouth to prevent smoke from pouring into my lungs. The high-pitched ringing of the alarm and the smoke punctuating the air were not helping.

"Ahhhh!!"

The sound of the bellowing scream peppered the air, but this time it was followed by a loud thud and boom. It felt like it was coming from the main floor.

What is that sound? I continued to edge down the hallway. I wanted to speed up, but there was no knowing where the stairs might drop off. The floor was carpet and so were the stairs, so it was hard to tell the line between the two.

"Ahhh!" This time it was followed by a deep, muffled thud. *"Ahhh!"* Then a larger thud. The sound of something large hitting the ground could be heard downstairs, along with large, heavy footsteps sprinting along the creaky floorboards.

"Kerry! Stop! You need to calm down!" I was hearing my mother call out from downstairs.

I edged my way toward the stairs and saw a light bending around the corner. I sprinted down the stairs and stopped short of the landing; I was met by the picture of the microwave on fire. Smoke was rising from the back of the microwave and starting to make its way around to the rest of the kitchen.

"Kerry!" I could hear my mother scream from around the corner. "Kerry, you need to calm down! Please set it down!"

I sprinted down the remainder of the stairs and came into view of the rest of the kitchen. The microwave continued to blaze and my father could be seen on the opposite side of the room with a look of horror and dismay on his face. He looked mortified as he stared into the fire that kept growing. He was holding two knives close to his body. One was tucked against his hip, pointed toward the fire, in his left hand. His right hand was extending a larger butcher's knife that pointed in the direction of the fire.

"Ahhhh!!" He continued to panic as the fire got bigger and the alarm screamed on.

"Kerry! You need to calm down! It's OK. It's just an electrical fire. I need you to put the knives down so I can put the fire out," my mother, in distress, screamed. I peered around the corner and could see Mom in a staggered stance, a worried expression on her face.

My father continued to scream. Everything was at a standstill. The fire continued to rage and grow larger. My mother frantically scanned the room and couldn't move forward.

"Dad! Put the knives down!" I screamed.

The look on his face remained unchanged: horrified.

"Dad!" I screamed.

"Kerry!" My mother was yelling again. "It's OK! You need to calm down! I can fix this! Just put down the knife."

The alarm continued to blare, along with the fire. The phone could barely be heard, but it was ringing in the background.

A large sound could be heard from outside, along with a view of the exhaust output. The smoke was beginning to fill the house; it was becoming harder to see. My eyes were watering and I could feel smoke sneaking past my hand and beginning to burn my lungs.

"Dad! We need to leave!" I continued to yell in his direction.

Nothing. He was paralyzed by fear.

"Kerry, you need to relax! I'm just going to move past you to disconnect the microwave from the power outlet." My mother took a cautionary step forward as her eyes traced my father's flinching movements.

Her feet quietly skimmed against the floor as the crackling from the fire screamed out. Sparks from behind the microwave illuminated the room.

I directed my attention back to my mother. She was now standing directly next to my father. He continued to stare, a look of horror at the towering fire.

"Kerry?" My mother said as she placed her hand against his shoulder.

I blinked as a moment of darkness encapsulated my eyes for what felt like two minutes. No more screaming, no more bright, strobe-like lights . . . no screeching noises, nothing—just silence. I could feel my chest slowly grow as I took a deep inward breath.

The crackling of the fire burrowed itself into my ears as the surrounding environment now ripped at my eyes. I opened my eyes, now in a dazed state.

An electrical pulse carved its way down my spine and into my legs. My legs collapsed from the impulse.

My father stared at the fire, still horrified, as I saw my mother standing upright next to him. Lodged underneath her chin and sticking out was a large metal handle. A red liquid smoothly flowed from under her chin toward the bottom of the handle. The liquid slowly fell to the ground in drops . . . then a stream . . . then a torrent.

"Mom!" I screamed out.

She slowly turned her head as I locked eyes with her. Her eyes dilated, red and bloodshot. She slowly closed her eyes and smiled faintly. She wavered back and forth and then . . . collapsed.

"Mom!" I screamed. "Mom!"

I sprinted over to her body, now static. "Mom!"

I slid into her as I pulled her body close to my torso.

"Mom!!" Tears immediately welled in my eyes and streamed down my face. I moved her head onto my lap and looked into her eyes. The

black and metal handle jutted from the underside of her mouth. She opened part of her mouth in an effort to breathe, and the gleam of the knife from inside her mouth shined against the fire's fury.

The image burned itself in my mind. She blinked sporadically as she lifted her hand from the ground.

"Mom, what do I do?! Tell me what to do!" I screamed.

I looked up at my father. He was still standing in a panicked position, staring at the fire. His eyes remained locked on the blaze. "What the fuck are you doing?! Help me!" I screamed, completely in panic. *"Please!!"* Tears were streaming down my face as I tried to scream out the words. *"Dad!!"*

I extended my hand and tugged against his pajama bottoms.

A clean and crisp feeling of a blade moving through skin reverberated throughout my right forearm. In shock, I looked down at my forearm. In one swift movement, he swung the knife, still pointed at the fire. I could feel the heat from the fire and the oxygen in the air tugging at my arm. The feeling of swift metal piercing my skin just below my right hand and then swiftly pulling out.

"Ahhhhh!" I screamed as my hand went limp. Immediately, I pulled back my hand and stared at the fresh cut. I raised my forearm to my mouth and tried to bite the cut to stop the bleeding. The taste of iron and phlegm engrossed every sensation in my mouth.

A loud thud hit the front door across from the kitchen. "This is the fire department! We're coming in!" Two loud thuds, followed by the fall of the door echoing across the room. Two large men in fire suits entered the room and looked around, assessing the situation. The larger of the two, in front, looked toward the kitchen with the fire and glanced back at the other man.

"Alright! Everyone out now!" the larger man screamed.

The two men took a step forward and peered into the kitchen. The firefighters looked toward my father and then back at my mother and me. "Oh, my god," said the first. He looked at us and then peered back at the fire. "Get him out of here!" screamed the first man—seemingly in panic for such a large, commanding man—as he scanned back and forth between me, my father, my mother, and the fire.

Two firefighters sprinted from behind the first fireman and toward me. Swiftly, two hands latched onto my shoulder and pulled me backward.

"Wait! Wait! I need to help my Mom!" I screamed in panic. It was all I could think.

The firefighters lifted me to my feet and hoisted me toward the door. "Let me go, you piece of shit. Let me help my mom!" I kicked my feet in fury as the blood from my wrist streamed down the back of the firefighter's back.

"Leave now!" said the firefighter in the back.

The firefighter quickly turned toward the door as the scene burned itself into my eyes. . . . My father standing in a paralyzed terror . . . my mother bleeding out on the ground . . . a kitchen on fire . . . two firefighters cautiously approaching. The memory of the end—the memory of a new beginning.

The firefighter carried me to the door of my house and lowered me to the ground. "Please, I need to help my mom. Let me go, asshole!" The firefighter continued to squeeze my right wrist, causing more and more blood to flow out against his fire jacket. A paramedic grabbed my arm and turned my body toward her. "Stop flailing, and let the firefighters do their job," she said in tense tones. "The more you intervene, the less likely the chance that we will be able to save your mom and dad! Do you understand?"

I turned my head back to the fire. One firefighter was within steps of my father while the other was trying to attend to my mom on the ground. Her face rolled toward mine as her eyes stared off into the distance, lifelessly.

"Get off me!" I screamed as I ripped my bloody arm from the paramedic and sprinted back inside the house. *"Mom!"* I screamed into the fury of the fire and the alarm.

My father blinked his eyes rapidly and met mine. *"Mom!"* I screamed again.

The firefighter closest to my father rapidly grabbed him, spun him around, and slammed him into the adjacent counter.

"Get that kid out of here!" screamed a voice in the distance.

A hand clenched itself to my left hand and grasped tightly. "Let go of me!" I screamed. Two more firefighters entered the house, hoisted themselves under my arms, and lifted me, carrying me from the house. "Please, please, let me go! She needs my help. *Please!*" Tears streamed down my face as my eyes blurred anything I was seeing in the distance.

"Please," I pleaded once more as I was being carried outside. With each lumbering step, the flare from the kitchen fire became smaller and smaller. I frantically looked around the neighborhood and could see people standing outside on their porches. "What are all of you doing? Go help her . . . please!" I screamed in utter distress. The two firefighters carried me to an ambulance and placed me on the metal ledge of the back. Immediately, as I felt the cold metal embrace my back, I jolted my legs awake in an attempt to sprint back inside the house. To no avail. I was met with the stern hold of the two firefighters. The firefighter on the right, the bulkier of the two, raised his face shield. I was met by two vivid blue eyes.

"Kid, listen to me. Right now, we have a fire that could possibly spiral out of control. If the fire grows to a point in which it hits a natural gas line, then the whole house can go up. You will lose your mom and your dad and I will lose men I care about. Do you want to be responsible for the deaths of everyone here?"

"I . . ."

"No, you don't. So stop this right now and let us do our job. We will get your mom and dad out of the house before that scenario can unfold." His eyes remained locked on me. Briefly, he peered into the back of the ambulance, nodded, lowered his face shield, and then took off in the direction of the house.

A hand lowered to my shoulder. I turned slowly as tears poured down the sides of my face.

"Sir, my name is Clara. How do you feel? Is anything hurting?"

Without saying a word, I tearfully looked toward my wrist. Blood was flowing out at a fairly fast rate. The skin was cleanly cut; there was no shearing or tearing on any side.

"Alright. We need to get that fixed up." She turned her body toward the back of the ambulance and reached into various compartments. "Sweetheart, I need you to move up here so I can insert an IV."

I continued staring in the direction of the house. The pulsing of light flickered against the window in the main room of the house.

"Sir?"

"I'm not moving from this position. I need to see . . . " I was adamant in my tone.

That's the moment Clara lowered herself onto the metal ledge next to me. "OK. Well, if that is the case, I am going to need to see your arm."

Without any more questions, I extended my arm in her direction, all while keeping my eyes locked on the house.

Clara poured alcohol over the cut. The stinging sensation was nothing compared to the screaming inside my head. *I need to get back into the house! I need to see if Mom is alright! I need to punch Dad. I need to . . .*

"Sweetheart, what's your name?" Clara asked.

"Sam." I answered swiftly, determined.

"Alright, Sam," Clara said. "I understand that I am probably the last person on the planet that you want to be talking to right now. But there is something that you need to know. The men and women who are in the house right now are professionals. This is what we do on a daily basis. I know you want to be helping out—to be helping your mom and dad. As it stands right now, you are losing a lot of blood. If you don't stop moving and shuffling around, you might pass out."

A boom shook the inside of the truck. An explosion rang out from inside the house and a huge flicker of light illuminated the main window.

"Mom!!" I scream.

I rip my hand from Clara. With all the energy I have left in my legs, I push against the concrete below and take off in the direction of the house.

"Sam!" Clara screamed.

The air brushed against my face as I vaulted the police line. I was then met by the soft sensation of grass against my feet.

"Ughhh!" I exhaled forcefully as my view of the house started to blur. The sensation in my legs flooded outward and I felt a tingle against the back of my spine. "What's *happening!?*" I screamed.

My legs collapsed against the soft, dewed grass. My vision blurred as my sight compressed into tunnel vision. All the energy seeped out of my arms and legs and my chest collapsed against the grass. My face, now resting against the grass below, stared up at the steps leading to my house. A firefighter sprinted out the front door, my mother in his arms. Her body limp, her eyes dull, blood cascading down the front side of her body—and seemingly all that blood absorbed by her white shirt.

"Mom!" I muttered, weakly.

Darkness engulfed my eyes and my body went limp.

FIVE

SILVER LINING

"Sam? Sam! Wake up, man."

I open my eyes to see Cam staring down at me sprawled across the waterfront bench.

I rub my eyes and look past his shoulder. The sky is a bright orange. "What time is it?" I ask.

"I'm not sure, but the sun is setting soon." Cam looks over his shoulder at the now pinkish-red sun pushing itself over the distant horizon.

I rub my eyes again and place both feet on the ground. I quickly glance under the bench to see if my pack is still there.

"Cam! Where is my pack?" I say, jolting upward.

I look over to see Cam smiling. "It's right where you left it, dummy. You just weren't looking all the way."

Cam points down to the side of the bench my head was resting on and motions toward my large, brown backpack.

I take a deep breath and look over at him. "How'd you know I was down at the park?"

"I went over to where you were working and didn't see you anywhere. Mr. P was still there, running around in between cars and

53

smiling, but I couldn't find you at all. Knowing you, I figured if you had any spare time you'd come down to the waterfront."

"Guess you know me pretty well, then," I say as I laugh and punch him in his shoulder.

He chuckles for a second, then lets out his own deep laugh. "Know you? Son, I know you better than you think."

"Guess so," I say as I look around.

No more kids in the fountain. It seems everyone has retreated to their homes.

"What's wrong?" Cam asks as he looks over at me.

I sigh. "Nothing. There were just some kids playing in the fountain earlier, and it seemed like they were having a blast. I kind of hoped they were still here. Something felt refreshing about seeing them laugh and smile."

I look back at Cam and see him clamping his stomach.

"You hungry?" I say as he makes a slight grimace with his face.

"Hungry?! Son, I didn't get to eat all my Salisbury steak because you were causing a ruckus at the shelter at lunch! Yes, I'm hungry."

I smile a bit but can see Cam is visibly annoyed.

"Well, I don't know what to tell you," I say. "I didn't really have the best day working the streets. So, I have no money as it is right now."

"What!" Cam is exasperated. "You told me that you had a good feeling about making money today!"

I look at Cam, annoyed. "Well, sorry. How about you? Did you make any money today?"

Cam's face changes from vexation to annoyance . . . and then he smiles. "Shit," I say as I reach down into my pack.

"Sam, don't cuss!" Cam says as he leans over the bench to see what I'm reaching for. "What are you looking for anyway?"

I keep digging around in my bag, hoping to find a small black portable compartment.

"I'm looking for my money bag," I answer as, finally, I touch it. "Ahh, nice." I pull out the bag, unlace the twine holding it together, and peer inside.

"So . . . what?" Cam asks. "Do we have enough goodies to go get some food?"

I look up at him in despair. "No, we're all out of money." I flip the bag upside down. All that falls out is a piece of black lint.

"You know what this means?" Cam says, all depressed.

"Yeah," I say as I nod in agreement.

"Well, let's go check, then. Grab your pack and we'll check around the park."

I grab my bag from under the bench and once again heave the thing onto my back.

"Dang," Cam says. "I was really hoping for a big ol' filet of fish. And maybe some fries. Oh, and maybe a big ol' Coke to send me on my merry way."

My stomach is starting to toss and turn. It growls the more Cam talks about food.

"Or maybe getting a Big Mac and some apple slices. And a big glass of water and Hi-C. Dang, that sounds good."

My stomach is screaming in unison with every word related to food that Cam utters. "Cam, please shut up. You're making me starving." I try to squeeze my stomach to make it stop.

"Good! Now you know how hungry I am and how disappointed I am that we can't go get a pile of food! And I figured you might have enough money to put into your savings account today."

I look at him, disgusted. "Maybe if you stopped ragging on me and finally got some money of your own, then we wouldn't be in this position!"

Cam smiles and then lets out a deep laugh. "You're right, Sammy. If I could just feed myself I would, and if you could just protect yourself, you would. Am I right? But until we can both do these things, we're stuck together. So shut it, big man."

"Whatever . . . dick," I say, whispering the word under my breath.

"What was that, Sam?"

"Nothing, nothing," I say. "Let's just go fish some delicious food out of the garbage so we can stop our stomachs from being so vocal."

Cam nods in undesired agreement.

We split up around the park and search every trash can on the waterfront. They are mostly empty since the city picks up the trash on Tuesday, and it's now Wednesday. But there are some hidden treasures locked away. And by that I mean a half-eaten bag of Doritos and a turkey sandwich with the remainder of the crusts sealed inside a zip-lock bag.

"I hate when we have no money," I say to myself as I remove the top of a trash bin and peer inside. "Wow, what a find!" I say, dripping in sarcasm, as I remove a rotten banana peel covering a Slurpee cup with a little liquid left inside. I toss the banana peel back into the trash and suck down the remaining liquid. It tastes . . . nasty. Like someone left syrup rotting in the sun for a couple of days. "Ehh!" I scream as I gulp down the remainder. I wipe my face with my coat and then continue to forage for treasure. The rest of the trash is a disappointment. Nothing but paper scraps from some asshole too busy to recycle and a broken bottle of beer.

I search the rest of the park. Not much luck. All I can find are some orange peels and a couple of half-rotten apple cores.

"Damnit," I say, sighing. I stare at the sky. "Why can't the city collect trash on Thursday? That way I could at least have a decent meal!"

I walk back to the bench I was sleeping on and find Cam sitting, staring at the carousel. "What are you doing?" I ask him.

"Nothin' much. Just watching the lights on the carousel. They look beautiful against the sunset."

I briefly turn to look at the carousel, but I'm quickly distracted by my stomach screaming at me. I look up at Cam desperately. "You find any food?"

Cam shakes his head in disappointment. He too is squeezing his stomach trying to stop the pain. "Nah, I didn't find anything. Every trash can is empty. Dang city cleaner should show up a couple days later to help guys like us out."

I look toward the sunset and feel somewhat placated—only to be quickly reminded that I shouldn't waste energy doing anything but eating.

"Did you get anything?" Cam says, and now he's a bit excited.

"Not very much. I got a half-eaten bag of Doritos, a partial turkey sandwich with crusts, an orange peel, and some half-rotten apple cores."

Cam's eyes perk up and he gets excited. "Sounds better than

nothing! What do you want to eat since you found them?"

I look at him, disgusted. "This . . . this food . . . it's all disgusting. Besides the Doritos."

Cam is starting to salivate—literally salivate—with drool dripping out his mouth.

"What's wrong with you?" I ask as I watch a big gob of drool drop from his lips.

Cam doesn't stutter at all. He just looks starving. I look down at my magnificent collection. "How about I just take the Doritos and you can have everything else?"

Cam smiles, pleased. I hand him the mess of garbage. He cups his hands together and motions me to drop everything in. I sigh for a moment and then drop the food into his hands.

In one quick motion, he throws everything in his mouth, takes three large chews, and then I watch as his Adam's apple moves up and down.

"Gross!" I say as he licks his lips and wipes his face with his green jacket.

I survey our surroundings. There are no people in the park. The sun has gone past the horizon and flickers of red light stream over the mountains in the distance.

"What's the plan now?" I say to Cam as I keep looking for anyone around.

"Well, it's nightfall, and you know what that means!"

I sigh and look toward my legs. They finally feel good after a day of hauling that pack around. It doesn't matter, though—they are gonna hurt a lot more later.

"Yeah, I know what it means," I say as I kick a rock between a crevice in the pavement.

"Good," he chuckles—and I can now see him eyeing my Doritos. "You gonna eat those?" Cam has been tracking the movement of the bag with his eyes. It is almost as if he is waiting for me to slip and drop the bag on the ground so he can quickly snatch it up and gulp it down.

"Where we gonna walk tonight?" I ask as he continues to follow the movement of the Doritos.

He stops and turns toward me. "I actually have a great idea . . . but

I won't tell you unless you give me those Doritos."

"Cam, just freaking tell me! I don't have time for this shit," I say, my tone completely irritated.

"This is me simply offering a trade. A bag of Doritos for a very valuable idea." He smiles and continues to follow the bag with his eyes.

"Whatever," I say as I toss him the bag.

Cam's face lights up and he almost catches the damn thing in his mouth. He immediately crushes the bag and then drains all the chip fragments into his mouth.

"Well." I'm crossing my arms and tapping my foot on the pavement.

"One second, one second," he says as he lifts the bag upside down and hits the sides to ensure no stray piece is left behind. He hits the bag once more and then brings the bag opening to eye level to peer inside.

He sighs briefly and then crushes the bag in his hand and shoves it in his pocket.

"Well," I say, the rate of my foot tapping increasing.

Cam chuckles, smiles. "My bad. I forgot you were there." He laughs again. "My idea is pretty simple. You know those buildings downtown that are linked to the block by those alleyways?"

"Yeah," I say, questioningly.

"Well, in the alleyway, those buildings all have fire escapes leading to the roof. If we can climb the fire escapes, haul our stuff up there, and keep from being seen, we'll be safe. Also, we won't have to walk around downtown all night hoping not to get rolled or stabbed."

"Cam . . . that's actually a really good idea. Not a lot of people are limber enough to follow us up there. And even if they did see us, we would probably hear them coming up the steps."

I look over at Cam sitting on the bench. He looks tired and still very hungry.

"What's the matter?" I ask as he looks at his hands.

He lets out a big sigh. "If only I hadn't eaten all the Doritos in one bite, then I might still have some food left over."

I roll my eyes and start to walk in the direction of downtown, with its alleys interlacing the streets. *Cam actually has a great idea.* If we pull this off, then maybe I can get a normal day's sleep in and put more of my time into working the streets tomorrow. And by working the streets I mean making enough money that I actually have something to eat instead of orange peels and rotten apples.

It's dark now. The sun has finally collapsed over the hills and night is beginning to take its place. I hate night. When I was little, I was morbidly afraid of the dark. The looming monsters, the boogeyman, and that ominous closet of endless possibilities. But Mom would always come in and comfort me and the fears would subside. She would grab my hand, stroke my right arm, and tell me everything was going to be alright. It gave me peace. The serendipity of finding peace after fear. The only problem on the streets is no one comes to save you. Plain and simple: if you are sleeping at night and someone is not watching your back, the boogeyman and his friends find you. If they find a person sleeping, they "roll" that person. Beatings, stabbings, dismantling anything to get a person's possessions. There is no release from the fear—there is only walking to avoid the tremors of fears.

I look up at the night sky. There are no stars. The street lighting and pollution from the city block them out.

"Bummer," I mutter under my breath.

"What's wrong?" asks Cam as he looks up, hoping to see whatever I've been looking at. "I don't see anything. Only blackness—and an image in my head of Salisbury steak."

I look over at him and smirk. "Are you ever *not* thinking of food? Like, is there ever a moment where you are just chilling?"

"Well . . . " He thinks to himself for a moment. "No . . . not really." Cam smiles and continues to rub his hands together. I imagine he's thinking about every piece of food that he can imagine.

I let out a heavy breath.

"I do care if you're safe, though," Cam says, as he looks at me intently.

I briefly stumble over a crack in the sidewalk. "You *what*?" My tone is one of exasperation.

He lets out a big, bellowing laugh and points his head forward. "Ever since I met you at the orphanage. When it was your 'break time,' or whatever you used to call it. I remember seeing you sitting in the corner of the yard. You always had a flushed face, like something had been taken from you and there was no way of getting it back. You looked alone. Like a boy who saw fear. Like a boy who saw death."

I immediately shove my hands in my pocket and start to pick up the pace. My pack is starting to feel heavier. My heart is beginning to race; I can feel my face freeze up.

"But there was something interesting about you." Cam says this from behind me.

I bury my face in my jacket. I feel an anxiety attack coming. *Bum . . . bum-bum . . . bum-bum . . . bum-bum-bum.* Faster and faster. I can hear my heart making revolutions.

"Like someone was always with you." Cam says this and then stops in place.

Hot. I feel hot. It's still warm outside from the summer air, and I feel like I am burning alive. I rip my body back toward Cam.

"Cam! Enough! I don't want to hear anymore. Don't talk about *them*, don't ever talk about them, and don't talk about me like you know me!" I scream these words as I feel tears welling in my eyes. "You will never understand! You will never understand what it's like to walk in and see . . . *that* . . . to see life dangling by a thread. A damn thread is what stood between an asshole and a monster!"

I sink to my knees and can feel the tears pouring down my face. I still feel hot, my chest heavy. There is no air to breathe, only the humidity.

Cam takes his bag off his back and places it on the ground. He sighs deeply and places his hand on my shoulder. It feels heavy and burdensome.

"I'm sorry," Cam says. "I'm sorry for everything that you have been through. But you need to know something."

I look up at his bearded face and watch him stare at me intently. "That time has passed now. Sadness: it'll only make you weak. It makes you vulnerable. And you can't be vulnerable here. This city, and these people, will beat you to your knees if you let them."

Tears continue to stream down my face. I am hyperventilating, subtly. My chest feels full and heavy. It's hard to gain composure when you can barely breathe.

I'm trying to focus on my breathing, but Cam's voice is playing in the background.

"Take deep breaths and regain your composure," Cam says, placing his other hand on my shoulder. "If someone sees you, they'll take advantage of you when you're like this."

"This is weird," I say and let out a small laugh.

"What's weird?" he says as he pulls me to my feet and brushes the dirt off my shoulders.

"Nothing. Nothing," I say.

I brush the tears from my eyes and let out a brief smile.

"Whatever, man," Cam says. "Let's get moving. We need to find a good fire escape."

SIX

PEACE

Cam and I are walking through downtown.

"Cam, what time is it? I'm exhausted." I'm watching myself drag my feet forward inch by inch.

Cam looks up as though he can read the night sky. "It's gotta be pretty late," he says as he points to the moon directly over our heads.

I sigh. My brief nap wasn't enough to curb the fatigue and all my aches. Everything is sore. Everything hurts. But this isn't unusual. Every day is a marathon. I just hoped that the days would get easier with time. It's funny how they don't. When a person is little, they notice that their body adapts to stress, making the load easier as you go. Out here, it's different. There's no coping, no getting accustomed to the stress. It's always hard.

"Let's try this alleyway here," I say as I point to a small entryway located around the corner from an old Chinese food joint.

I look over at Cam, waiting for a response. His eyes are locked on the Chinese food shop.

"Cam, you're starting to drool again," I say as I watch a big gob of saliva roll out from his cheek and nest itself in his dark beard.

"Yeah," he says as he licks his lips and inhales deeply through his nose. "What I wouldn't give . . . "

"Nope! We're not doing this again!" I say as I bark back at Cam. "Last time you did this, both of us ended up starving. I don't want to go through the pains of knowing nothing is in there."

Cam sighs. "You're probably right. It will only make things worse for both of us if I look at it, and talk about it, and dream about it, and think about it, and imagine about it, and . . . "

Cam looks over at me while finishing the last "about it." I have a stern look fixed on him. He sighs and looks at the ground. "Fine," he says as he kicks a piece of glass on the ground with his tattered boots.

We round the corner and peer down the alley. It's about 500 feet from the start of the alley to the outlet on the other end. It's dark, damp. Steam can be seen rising out of vents from the basements of the buildings on both sides. Dumpsters line both sides followed by little steps to small doors with bars on the window frames of each door.

"Wow, this looks really creepy," I say, looking at Cam. "Like somewhere someone might get stabbed." I shudder.

His face is cocked forward and continues to glare down the alley. "Just keep your hand on your shiv," he says as he takes a step forward.

We take a few first steps into the alley. "Hello?" I call, hoping for no response. I am met by a honking horn around the outlet at the alley's other end, and a reverberation of the sound bouncing between buildings.

"This isn't getting any less creepy," I whisper to Cam, tightening my grip on the shiv in my pocket.

Thud!

"Ahh! What the fuck!" I scream as both Cam and I jump in the air. I whip my shiv from my pocket and point it in the direction of the sound. We both immediately turn to find a cat on top of the garbage can trying to paw his way into a closed-up box of Chinese food.

"Huh?" I say as I feel my heart skip and beat. My face feels flush and my feet are ready to run.

I look over at Cam. He looks flustered too. Neither of us likes being here. This alley is . . . creepy, unpredictable, concealed . . . in a word, terrifying. Everything about it screams unknown.

"Sam! Let's grab that Chinese food!" Saliva begins dripping down the side of Cam's mouth. He turns his body toward the cat and slowly begins walking forward. His hands are clenched in a claw formation.

"Cam," I croak with a deep voice. Cam turns his head back; his face is completely flush. "I don't care about the food. I just want to go to bed."

Cam lets out a large exhale—clenches his fists—and turns around. "Fine! We need to find a fire escape", Cam says as he turns back to look farther down the alley. "I think there is one about fifty yards down."

We continue to walk through the alley. *What do they even keep down there?* I think, cringing. I can feel a shiver down my spine.

"Hey, that might actually work," I say to Cam as I look up at a fire escape beginning fifteen feet above the ground. "The only problem is we can't reach it, even if you hoist me up."

The fire escape is laid out simply. The initial ladder—those fifteen feet up—branches into four alternating flights of stairs between four levels.

"Yeah, this definitely was not made for the action of climbing up and down," Cam says. Jagged pieces of rusted iron jut out from the sides.

"I guess that means we get to climb it," I say, letting out a brief chuckle of uneasiness.

"Quiet, Sam. We need to find a way up there." Cam walks to the wall to see if there is anything we can get a handhold or foothold on so we can climb. The wall looks slick. The moisture from the vents has coated it in greenish-brown slime. Cam places his hand against the slime, rubs it between his fingers, and lets out a sigh of disgust. "Well, there is no way that we can climb this." He tries to wipe the slime off on the pavement. Unsuccessful, he wipes it off on his torn black pants.

"I'm not even touching that," I say as I almost gag watching Cam rub it between his fingers. I look around the alley. Still creepy, still scary, and still somewhere I don't want to be. "Why can't we go to The Split tonight?" I ask Cam.

"I overheard someone at the shelter today saying that Ol' Betty was sleeping with her friends there the other night and she got rolled," Cam says as he continues looking up at the fire escape.

"She seemed fine to me at the shelter," I answer.

"She was able to fight the guys off, but only barely. Even with the help of her friends. That's why she seemed so jumpy today and had her hand cocked against her boot."

I sigh and continue to look around. "Hey, I have an idea." I point back down the alley at one of the Dumpsters.

Cam tracks my finger and follows the line to the Dumpsters. He smiles at me and nods in agreement. We walk toward the large trash containers and position ourselves for pushing. "We need to be quiet so the restaurant owner doesn't hear us and call the cops," I say as we prepare to brace ourselves for the weight. Cam nods.

"One . . . two . . . *three*," Cam says as his face turns red against the weight of the Dumpster. The thing slowly moves as we heave it down the alleyway. It screeches bit by bit as we continue to push. The Dumpster has wheels, but they're broken along the axles and aren't helping much.

"Hey! Who the hell is out here!" screams a voice from behind a nearby door that has opened. It's English, but has a staccato, heavily accented ring to it.

"Sam! Hide! Quick!" Cam says as he dives into one of the stairways and lines himself up to blend in with one of the doors. I look around and quickly decide the best course of action is to hide behind the out-valve on one of the steam vents.

A short, white-haired man darts out from the side door of the Chinese restaurant and turns his head both ways. He mutters something in Chinese and raises his hands in the air. He walks over to the Dumpster and kicks the side of it hard. He screams something—also in Chinese—and then walks back to the door. A brief moment of silence is followed by a loud slam.

"Sam, we need to go quickly," Cam says as he takes a brief step out of the door well.

"No, let's just go," I say to Cam as I push myself off the ground, covered in dust and glass. I look down at my hands and they're covered in grime and what looks like tar. "This place is gross. We should leave," I say as I try to wipe my hands against my jacket.

"Do you wanna be dirty and have a good place to sleep, or be clean and get stabbed?" Cam asks, angrily, as he positions himself behind the Dumpster.

I let out a heavy sigh and try to get the residual grime off my hands. "So gross," I say to myself as I place my hands against the back of the Dumpster. I exert all my body weight into the Dumpster while Cam does the same. It begins to move again—and the screeching resumes with it.

"Stop," Cam says, looking at the large container. "Let's push lower so it's not so loud." I look down at the Dumpster and there are small grooves on the lower half to facilitate lifting by the garbage truck. "That groove will help us heave," Cam says, brushing sweat off his forehead.

We both position our bodies against the Dumpster, this time lower and angled inward. It slowly starts to move again. This time, it's much quieter. The wheels aren't nearly as loud, and it doesn't screech.

"It's working," I say, keeping my voice low. We continue giving it our full exertion.

We finally get it to the area under the fire escape. "Alright," says Cam, standing up and breathing hard. "Climb up there and let me know how it goes."

"What? Why don't you go first?" I say as I look at how unstable the Dumpster is. "And the ladder might collapse from my weight!"

"Stop being a baby," Cam says as he pats the top of the Dumpster.

I grit my teeth and let out a sigh. *This is gonna suck,* I think. I climb on the big container by using one of the grooves on the bottom and inching myself around the perimeter. One of the Dumpster's housings is broken and has caved in on the left-hand side. "This feels really unstable," I say to Cam as I extend my hands to maintain balance.

"Just hurry!" Cam says as places his hands on the Dumpster to assure me it isn't going to collapse.

I edge my way toward the part of the Dumpster the ladder is underneath and reach up for a strong handhold. I put some of my body weight on the ladder and hope the structure doesn't fall. No sounds can be heard. It feels pretty stable. I place my other hand on the ladder and hoist the rest of my body weight up. My backpack is about thirty pounds—and it feels like hauling an extra body upward. I swing my legs and position them on the lowest ladder bar.

"How you doing?" Cam calls up, in a whispering voice, from below.

"I could definitely be better," I say as I continue to climb the rest of the ladder. I now reach the flights of stairs and cross the flat levels that connect them as I continue moving up. The windows in each of the rooms on the levels are dark. There are apparently no residents at all. The building looks abandoned. "Cam, there is no one here!" I say as I look down to see him climbing up on the Dumpster. The big container doesn't screech when he gets on. I chuckle for a second.

"You must be so fat that the Dumpster is pinned on the ground from your weight," I say.

Cam looks up at me. His face is flushed red from the exercise, and he looks pissed. "Shut up, Sam! And be quiet. We don't know if anyone is still in the alley."

I chuckle again and then continue to work my way up the altering flights of stairs. Level by level the windows are either barred or boarded shut. It's a wonder this fire escape is even standing. The building itself looks like it should be demolished.

After climbing the four alternating sets of stairs with jagged and sometimes sketchy railings, I finally reach the top. Well, the top of the staircases. There is still one remaining ladder that leads to the roof. "How far down are you?" I say to Cam as I place my foot on the first ladder rung.

"I'm coming, you speed demon. Just go up to the top and wait for me!"

I turn to look back toward the ladder and start climbing. I peer over the top of the ladder. The roof is pretty dirty. Birdshit everywhere. A nice white aesthetic. And the dirt mixed in makes it look almost worse than the street below. "Cam, this roof is pretty gross," I whine, looking down at him.

"Doesn't matter! At least we'll be able to sleep!" he says, looking up and making a *shhhh* sign with his finger. He is rounding the final railing and dragging himself toward the ladder. He looks weathered, exhausted.

I hoist myself onto the roof and head toward the opposite edge. The city is . . . gorgeous. The lights beaming, cars slowly moving and intermingling with one another on the streets, various people walking to and fro. I close my eyes and take a deep breath.

"I could do it right now," I say to myself. "I could finally see her again. All the pain would stop and there would be nothing more to worry about." No food, no sleeping, no safety worries, I tell myself. It would be my *fin*.

A hand reaches out and places itself on my shoulder. "But that wouldn't be very fun now, would it?" Cam says as he grabs my shoulder and turns me around. "Besides, we all know you wouldn't wanna leave dear old me stranded on this roof."

Cam lets out a big bellowing laugh and then walks to the middle of the roof and throws his pack to the side. He immediately lays down and closes his eyes. "You know what?" he asks, placing his hands on his belly.

"What?" I say as I look over the edge to see neon lights filling the street below.

"I think this is the first time I have felt bliss. No worry about being jumped. No worry about not being able to sleep well. And no worry about feeling like I might die tonight."

"Yeah," I say as I lean against the two-foot-high enclosure surrounding the roof. I look up at the sky and the stars are finally beginning to show themselves, even after the city's lights have done all they can to drown them out.

"We should probably go to bed," Cam says as he yawns and rolls onto his side. He has laid out his sleeping bag, but in his fatigue, he's forgotten to actually get inside it.

"Don't you want to . . . ?"

He shushes me by waving his hand and then bringing the "shhh" sign back to his lips. Within seconds, he's snoring.

I smile as I let my back slide down the side of the enclosure. My eyes feel heavy, like they are going to collapse. *I should probably lay out my sleeping bag.* I try to get my body to move, but it is too tired, too sore. My body continues to slouch until it hits the ground, and I extend my legs. The ground feels cool.

Everything feels excellent. For once. Everything feels right. For once. There is finally silence. There is finally a minuscule drop of peace.

SEVEN

PREDACIOUS NIGHTFALL

"Sam!" A voice cries out, seemingly from inside my head. Then my eyes snap open.

"Oh, you're awake now, are you? Well, what fun would this be if you weren't?" The man speaking is chuckling to himself and licks his lips.

He is grabbing my cheeks and holding them together.

He has a sharp silver knife pressed between my lips.

"Here's how this is going to work, big man. You scream, you shout, if you even breathe wrong, I'm gonna gut your cheek. Oh, and it won't be slow. I will make sure to make a nice ol' mark so people will definitely stare."

He takes the knife out from my lips, licks the flat edge, and laughs to himself. His breath smells horrible. My eyes are watering from the smell alone. When he smiles, I can see decay throughout his mouth. His teeth are rotting from the inside out.

"Maybe we should start with an introductory mark. You know, just so you know where we stand with things."

My face goes flush and my heart starts to pound. I can feel my legs go numb from fear. My body won't move; my arms just sit there by my side. I try to get some words out, at least enough to wake up Cam—but nothing.

The man takes the knife and places the warm blade an inch above my right eyebrow. He covers my mouth with his hand and presses the blade into my skin.

"Ahh!!!!!" I scream, but it is muffled, mitigated by the man's hand. My eyes are starting to tear up. I can feel my nerves—one by one—being exposed to the air. It is torturous.

He relieves his pressure on the blade. I can feel my warm blood starting to drip down my face. The blood is branching into deltas. One running over my eyebrow and in front of my eye. Another trailing off the side along my hair. And a final one pooling in the small divot of my temple. Tears, which are now streaming down my face, are mixing with the blood and leaking off my chin.

The man pulls the blade away and licks the flat edge. My heart starts to race faster. *What does this man want with me?* He releases his hand from over my mouth.

He takes the knife and wipes it along his coat and pant leg.

"What do you want with me?" I shudder. The man just looks down at the knife to make sure it is clean.

"Oh, boy! Isn't that a fun question?" He chuckles. I look over toward the opposite side of the roof and see Cam. He is laying there motionless. *Is he dead? Which one of us was this lunatic after from the start?* I turn my eyes back to the man, and he has been glancing in the direction I was looking. He lets out a deep, bellowed laugh.

"No one is going to save you, boy. It's just me and you up on this roof." He lets out a big laugh and his rotten breath flows out and fills the area around him. It is so bad it makes my cut burn.

"You ask why? Well, I'll tell you why. Today at the shelter. You were the one who grabbed that boy in the food line, correct?"

I nod slowly, wrapped in complete fear.

"Well, when you grabbed that boy and tried to lift him off his feet, that made me feel a certain way. The type of way that makes you feel really, really good inside. So, me not knowing who you were, I wanted to get a better look at you. And let alone, my luck, my chance occurred. You walked right up to me trying to grab some bread. That was when I decided it was meant to be."

My heart sinks. I knew I had seen and smelled this nasty breath before. It was the man who was standing near the bread cart at the East Hills Shelter.

"So, what did I do when I knew it was meant to be? I departed from my normal group. I followed you all day. I saw all of it! The conversations, you being ridiculous trying to get money Mr. P's way. I even saw you when you were sleeping in the park by the waterfront. But no, I couldn't have my fun then! There were too many people around who would spoil the fun."

He smiles and lets out a devious laugh. Again, his breath is so bad it makes my cut burn more.

"So, if I wasn't going to be able to have you in the park with all the delicious little kiddies around, then where was I going to have you?"

I moan in sheer terror. The more I scream, the tighter his disgusting hand clamps on my face. I look into his eyes and only see one thing: bloodlust. He takes the knife that he has been wiping on his coat and jacket and places the flat edge against my cheek. He slowly bends toward my cheek and licks the opposite flat edge. I close my eyes, again in sheer terror. His breath is still punctuating the air and making me want to vomit and cry.

I try to turn my head away, but he can feel the muscles in my neck flex. The second I try, he immediately cocks my head back.

"So, what was I to do?" he says as he smiles and flips the warm, moist saliva-dense knife onto my cheek. My body is filled with terror.

"When you woke up at the park, I saw you running around, hunting for some garbage so you could eagerly devour it. Then I saw you come up with this brilliant plan. What was it, see?" He appears to think to himself for a second. "Oh yes—word for word: 'Let's climb up on the fire escape and escape the dangers of the night.'"

He laughs again and brings his lips right up to my ear. "How fucking smart of you. But guess what?" He takes a deep breath and blows into my ear.

I scream. Terror. Agony. I can feel my legs starting to rebound just a bit, though. I try to kick, but he has both my legs locked under him. I try slipping my hand into my pocket, but he has my other hand anchored.

"The beauty of it is, it's just you, me, and death up here." He smiles, chuckles once more.

I look over toward Cam. That's what he means. That was the death, and if the death wasn't for me, then it must be for . . .

My heart drops and tears begin swelling in my eyes, now gushing down. *Not Cam. There is no way.* I glance over Cam's way again and he is still stagnant, completely static on the ground.

No movement, no twitches. Just a lifeless body.

The man releases his hand from my arm and places it on my inner thigh. "Don't do anything stupi . . ." he starts to say and . . . I immediately punch his head as hard as I can to get him off me.

He falls to the side and clutches for his head. I immediately scramble to my feet and sprint toward the opposite side of the roof, with the ladder going down. I glance over toward Cam; his face is silent. No sign of life, no breath, just lifelessness.

I switch my head back to the ladder, take one large bound, and vault the two-foot cement enclosure of the roof. "Freedom," I sigh, averting my gaze toward the fire escape ledging below . . . But the sensation of falling does not follow. I am ripped back in the direction of the roof.

There's no way, I am thinking as I fall back onto the whitish-gray roof. *I didn't even hear him get up.*

I smash back into the ground and immediately the man launches himself on top of me. I kick and scream as hard as I can. He has both of my legs pinned to the ground, using his feet, and has one hand holding the knife while the other quickly reaches for my throat.

"I told you not to do anything stupid, boy, and I wasn't jokin.'"

The bloodshot in his green eyes . . . the look of death mirroring off his pupils. His greasy black hair falls in front of his face and he laughs voraciously. My eyes water from the stench of his breath as it encompasses me—the horrid nature of the breath makes me feel even more trapped.

He twirls the knife around in his hand and brings it to the edge of my mouth. In one swooping motion, he slices the right side of my lip until it reaches my back molar.

I immediately feel a warm substance gushing from my cheek. There is no pain, only warmth. I try to breathe out and it only makes the blood flowing out of my mouth exit faster.

The man gets off my legs and feet and stands up as he looks down on his trophy. "Now listen here, boy. You better cooperate the rest of the night, or you're going to have a big smile from cheek to cheek."

I roll to the side and place my head against the cold rooftop. I am at an angle to the surface in which the blood now starts to run from inside my cheek down to the top of my hairline. I can feel the pain beginning to set in. Bit by bit, the nerves in my cheek greet the surrounding air with a scream of pain. I move my tongue over to the cut and can feel it slide through and sit on the outside of my cheek.

I lift my head from the ground and notice the amount of blood that has swelled into a pool beneath my head. I can feel my heart drop. *There's . . . there's . . . so much blood.* I can feel my face go flush and chills shoot down my spine. My stomach turns and my veins feel as though ice is pumping through them.

"There's so much blood!" I scream as I now feel the air through my exposed mouth and cheek, air that burrows itself in. "There's so much blood . . . "

I try to breathe out as I feel my heart pound rhythmically and my eyes collapse under their weight.

"There is," says the man as he chuckles down at me from above . . . and then my eyes go dark.

"There goes the fun." I hear him say this faintly, in what seems like my subconscious.

My head collapses against the ground, and I feel my body go cold.

EIGHT

FERVENT PAIN

My face feels moist. I open my eyes to find myself sprawled across the ground.

A pool of blood surrounds my face. I blink a couple of times from the sunlight. I swallow and am met with a nasty taste. I immediately push myself off the ground and start to choke. The moment my cheek leaves the pool of blood, I can feel the air outside mixing with the air inside my cheek. Every choke is met by a howl of pain—followed by another choke.

I place my finger on the right side of my lip. I move it up and down and can feel the tissue buildup on both sides. As my finger glides over the cut on the outside, my tongue does so on the inside.

I sit up on my knees and look down at the blood. A body-shaped pool of it sits on the rooftop and seems to glare back at me in the reflection of the sun. It isn't until this point that I notice the heat of the sun encasing my body. It is warm now—too warm. I need to get off this roof and try to get this cut taken care of. I try to wipe the blood off my naked body, but can't seem to find a way to do it.

Cam! I think as I immediately turn my body around. I am now yelling hard enough to break the temporary seal of skin over my cut, which causes it to open and scream to the air once again.

"*Cam!*"

"*Ahh!*" I gurgle this sound as I scan the rooftop.

The rooftop seems barren. Not a soul to be seen. No Cam. No body, no backpack, no sleeping bag. I rise to my feet and hobble over to my clothes, which look as though they were thrown to the opposite side of the roof. My legs feel weak and timorous. I look down and notice I am limping. I slowly reach down to grab my pants and underwear, but can't find my shirt anywhere. I glance over the two-foot enclosure with my body leaning against the cool concrete. My shirt and a fragment of my jacket are hanging from a window ledge below.

"Damn it," I whisper as I try to keep my jaw clenched to avoid reopening the cut. I look around for my backpack and can't find a thing. "That asshole took everything," I say, and I can feel blood coming up the backside of my throat. Tears began to well in my eyes.

"I can't do this." My knees fall back to the roof and I rest on my knees. I try to close my eyes to block everything out. It's no use. It is hot, my cheek and forehead are screaming at the air to stop bothering the nerves, and I am broken. Tears stream down my face as I push myself up from the ground with my left hand and continue to clamp my jaw shut with my right.

I hobble to the enclosure and slowly lift myself over and onto the ladder leading down to the fire escape. I slowly place one foot before the other and climb down using one hand. Until now, if I removed my hand from my jaw, I immediately would scream out in pain and clamp it quickly again. But now I am working my way down the fire escape. One by one I move between the levels and limp down the alternating staircases.

I finally reach the lowest level. I lean over the railing and my eyes begin to tear up more. The Dumpster has been moved back to its original spot! I look around and there is nothing to help. There are no clotheslines, no gutters—nothing to brace the fall.

I hobble to the ladder and, one by one, work my way down the rungs. I get to the final leg and hold on with one arm while clamping the other to my jaw. Even with the extension of my body, it is still a nine-to-ten-foot drop. I have no shoes and my body feels like it is going to collapse if I hit the ground. I take my hand off my jaw to place it on the final ladder rung—to hang as low as I can, by two hands—and feel the jaw scream in agony. Blood begins gushing from the cut and simultaneously pours from my cheek while filling my mouth.

I immediately take my right hand back off the ladder rung and . . . "shit!" I scream out as my hand slips slightly. I look up and the only thing holding onto the ladder rung is my left hand middle finger. This one finger is supporting my entire body weight. I unclench my jaw and try to swing my hand up to the ladder rung, but in doing so lose the grip my finger had on the bar. I fall while . . . looking up at the blood-soaked rung of the fire escape ladder.

I close my eyes as I brace for impact. The first thing to touch are my bare feet, which immediately crumple and push the weight backward. The next feeling is the sound of my butt and back scratching against the asphalt while my head kicks back and smacks the pavement. Blood once again begins gushing from my cheek and forehead and brimming from my mouth.

I look up in a daze and am met by a swirling of the alleyway and sky joining in a dissonance of blurry lights and colors. I can hear horns honking in the background and feel blood dripping onto my face from the bloody fire escape rung above. Blood is now pouring from my mouth and I can feel it pooling in the divot of my neck.

"Ohh," I moan, crying out, as I try to lift my head from the ground. "Help me!" I try to scream once again as I lift my head slightly. I look toward the entranceway and exit of the alley, still in a daze, and see people walking. My bloody hand reaches out for a couple walking by.

A woman cups her hands over her face and screams as the man covers her eyes. He quickly pulls his cell phone from his pocket.

"911! I'm at the alleyway of Kerry and Melinda! There is a boy lying in a pool of blood in the middle of this alley. Send help quick!"

My hand collapses from the extensive weight of gravity and my head falls to the side as I fade into oblivion. The last image I see is the man and the woman running toward me as I watch my bloody hand fall back to the grimy pavement.

"It's so hot," I say as my head collapses to the ground . . . blackness encloses my sight.

NINE

GRAVITY

"Nurse? Where is the nurse?" mutters the doctor as the sound of a curtain being pushed away rings across the room.

The doctor looks to the left and the right. A look of befuddlement encompasses his face. A brief moment passes and I can hear footsteps scuffling back and forth down the hallway, accompanied by the sounds of running.

"I found her! I found her!" says a faint voice from well outside the room. "Clara was covering for Linda. She is just finishing charting for the code in "Trauma 3."

The doctor sighs and taps his finger on his clipboard while his heavy shoes thump against the lineoleum floor.

"I'm coming! I'm coming!" she yells back. Her panicked footsteps echo off the ER corridor. "Sorry, Dr. Patterson, I was covering for Linda while she is on break. I need to read the report for one second before I can update you."

The doctor sighs and continues to tap his feet, this time at a quicker pace. It is so loud, it is echoing to a point outside the room. "Clara, Linda is supposed to sign out to you before she goes on break. Please address that issue next time so the patient doesn't have to wait—especially in the ER."

"Yes sir," says Clara in a slightly muffled, clearly intimidated voice.

"Since Linda didn't sign out to you, I will update you on our current situation. We have a young man here, yet to be identified, nothing on his person, and he was picked up with multiple lacerations and contusions. A major laceration runs from his right lip to the upper part of his mandible. The laceration runs from the lateral end of his mouth, perforating several parts of the mucosa, and stops just shy of his mandibular ligament. A smaller laceration stretches down from the medial aspect of his forehead to his right orbit. A large burn can be seen running from his wrist all the way up to his right bicep—although this seems to have been a past injury. Multiple contusions are present around his glutes and inner thighs. All the issues have been addressed with gauze and suturing by the ER staff, and the patient is now resting. He should be waking up anytime now. I need you to talk to the patient and see if you can learn more about him."

"Yes sir," says Clara. Scribbling can be heard from the other side of the curtain. The curtain is brushed to the side. A brief silence follows the curtain's swift movement. A timorous step echoes against the linoleum floor. The curtain is brushed to the side even further.

The sound of a few footsteps pressing forward are heard in the distance. "Clara, what's wrong?" The doctor takes a step further into the room. "Do … you know this young man?"

"Umm… I am not quite sure but he looks…familiar. You said he has no identification, correct?"

The doctor ruffles what sounds like a few pages on his clipboard. "Umm, yes, that is correct?"

Clara takes a muffled step forward as her weight pushes up against the bed. "I think I know who this is…"

"How so?" The doctor questions from a position farther away from the bed.

"I think that this is … Sam Case. There was a massive fire that broke out in a suburb not too far from town. When I was working as an EMT to pay my way through nursing school last year, I was one of the first responders. Sam had a major laceration which pierced his interosseous artery." She walks over to the bed and rotates my wrist. "That's why he has this burn and scar on his right wrist." Clara takes a step forward and places her hand against my face—slowly moving it to the right and the left. "Yes…I am positive. This is Sam Case."

The doctor at the edge of the room remains silent for a moment. "Will you be able to remain objective?"

Clara sighs for a brief moment. "Of course, Dr. Patterson. What happened to him? His condition is unusual and extreme from someone coming from his area."

The doctor continues combing through some pages. "The paramedics picked him up in an alley outside of *Little China*. By the look of things, he was jumped, tried to resist, couldn't get away, and then was molested. Along with the lacerations, he has a broken thumb, a contusion over his lumbar spine, and significant contusions over the posterior aspect of his scalp. It looks as though he fell off something and hit the ground hard."

The doctor mutters something to himself and continues scraping through the pages.

From where I lay, I can feel the movement of Clara examining different aspects of my body.

The doctor continues taking notes and scribbling short passages. He also keeps tapping his foot. The sound of the cardiac monitor in the background mirrors the sound of tapping.

The doctor takes a step forward into the room and partially leans against the end of the bed frame. "Are you sure you can remain objective?" he asks again.

The weight of Clara's body moves off the bed. "Of course, Dr. Patterson. I will begin charting."

The doctor approaches Clara. "Clara, I don't mean to upset you more, but by his physical state, it is very likely that this young man is homeless. I can talk to social work, but our options for a long-term disposition are limited. In the mean-time, we will do everything we can to help him."

"*Cam!*" I scream as I jerk upward and a large beep on the cardiac monitor screams in the background. "Where's Cam?" I burst out. I rip open my eyes to see both the doctor and Clara terrified. The cardiac monitor in the background is roaring up and down, and I can feel my body heat up from the inside. The rush of heat slowly creeps its way into my cuts. I can feel both cuts—cheek and forehead—slowly start to open and leak blood again. I quickly look down at my arm. A needle, partially covered by a piece of medical tape extends out of my arm and into an IV. I reach down and rip the IV out of my arm. Blood begins pooling outward and onto the hospital blanket below.

"Code Grey!" the doctor yells out as he drops his clipboard to the floor. Clara runs to the opposite sides of the bed and pin my arms to the bed as I flail my legs and arch my back.

"Code Grey—ER Room 104. I repeat "Code Grey"—ER room 104. Security personnel respond" A voice booms over the hospital PA system.

Clara watches in horror as I survey the room, looking left to right. "Where is Cam?" I yell.

"Clara, don't let his arm get free!" as he grasps my right arm and right leg as hard as he can.

"Where is Cam! Is he dead?" I'm screaming, and I ferociously try to gyrate my body to get these two to let go. Blood is starting to seep through the gauze, and I can feel it dripping down my face and into my mouth, where it begins to pool.

"Sam! Calm down! We are trying to help!" Clara says as she struggles to restrain me. Two security personnel and a nurse dart bedside after emerging from behind the curtain. Both security personnel grab my legs while the nurse makes a beeline for the cabinet and pulls out a syringe with a large needle.

"Just tell me where Cam is!" I scream again while working hard to fight back the pain. Tears are streaming down my face and drop to the bed.

The nurse from the cabinet flicks the needle and two drops of a clear liquid fall to the floor. "Nurse, restrain him!" yells the doctor as he, Clara, and the security personnel struggle to hold my legs against the bed.

I scan the room. I am pinned. "Please, just tell me where Cam is. I need him! Please!" I am begging. Clara, the security personnel, and Dr. Patterson now have me restrained to the bed, and I am lifting my pelvis and contorting myself in every direction to get away.

"Sam, you need to calm down! We don't know who Cam is," Clara forcefully tells me. I keep trying to twist my body to escape. It is no use. I am pinned.

"Clara, you need to find Cam for me!" And then I notice something: her eyes widen from the realization that I have used her name. The doctor, nurses, and Clara have me locked down against the bed, each straining mightily to do so.

"Nurse! Restrain him now!" the doctor continues to yell. The nurse holding the syringe scurries across the room and inserts the needle into the IV connected to my arm.

"Cam . . . Cam . . ." I mutter as I feel my body go limp and the room slowly fade into darkness. "Please . . ." I find myself sinking back into the bed and the pressure exerted by the nurses and the doctor seems to dissipate.

My consciousness is fading when I hear this from a nurse: "God, I hate treating homeless people. It's always something. They never want to take treatment—too doped up on drugs and alcohol, I guess."

I hear another nurse laugh lightly. My eyes roll back.

TEN

INNER DEMONS

"Hey, big man! How we doing today?" muttered a voice from behind my shoulder as I worked to pick up some fresh grass clippings.

I turned my head over my shoulder to see Cam leaning against the edge of the fence, looking inward and turned my way. I sighed heavily for a moment.

"Oh, so it's one of those days, is it?" Cam chuckled to himself and started to smile. "Well, I bet your bad day can't top my bad day at all!" He said this as he kicked a pebble through one of the small dia-mond-shaped openings in the fence.

"Oh yeah?" I said in disbelief as I continued to shred the pieces of grass in my hand. "Well then, let's hear what made your day so damn shitty!"

Cam's face turned from a smile to a look of disgust. "Sam, you might be having a bad day, but ain't no reason you need to use those adjectives like that! You say 'shitty' and I hear 'disheartened.' Come on, man!"

I smirked briefly and then turned back his way. "Cam, just let me hear the damn story. You're gonna make my day worse if you keep lecturing me on the merits of language. You sound like my frickin' mom," I said as I dropped the pieces of grass and clapped my hands to ensure no seedlings remained.

Cam smiled and took a deep breath to pull in his thoughts. "Alright, so I woke up at The Split this morning. Do you know where that is?" He fiddled with the fence as he asked his question.

"Yeah," I sighed. "Jekyll wouldn't shut up about how great the place is during the night. Anything that a person could want—booze and drugs . . . he said The Split is the place to get it."

Cam's face changed from joking to a look of complete seriousness. "This Jekyll kid doesn't sound like he has his head on straight." Cam stopped fiddling with the fence and stared at me intently.

I sighed again. "Nah, he's not that bad. But he does keep getting caught for trying to sneak out."

"Oh yeah? And how is this Mr. Jekyll making his escapes into the safety of the night?"

I kicked the dirt around by my feet and sighed. I lifted my head back and stared at the sky while letting out a deep breath. "After being here for six months, I've been able to watch everything he has been doing—right and wrong."

Cam chuckled to himself as he resumed playing with the holes. "Alright, alright, Mister Experience. Tell me how you have studied your prey. Watched him develop and fail along the way."

"You make it sound like I'm going to eat him once he slips up," I said, a small chuckle escaping into the air.

"See, the day's not that bad if I can make you laugh," Cam said.

"You wish you could make me laugh. Most of the time the only thing that you're talking about is food."

"Speaking of . . . " Cam had a devious smile on his face.

"Once I'm about to get up to leave, I'll give you my leftovers from lunch," I said as I looked back at Cam, now starting to salivate. "I swear you only come here to talk about my escape and me giving you food."

"Well, you don't like to talk about anything else, and most of the time you're in a sour or foul mood, so I tend to stick with what keeps you talking," Cam said, now ruffling his beard.

I shrugged. "I just want out," I sighed, and I could feel my voice whimper at my own words.

"Well, it sounds like this Jekyll guy might be the key to you escaping," Cam said, pretending as if he really didn't want to find out more.

"Yeah, but he is doing everything wrong. He has one plan and one plan alone. There is no contingency, no plan B, no nothing. If he makes it, he is going to make it on a whim."

Cam had an inquisitive look and ruffled his beard again. "So, you are saying that if he sets up contingencies or this 'plan B,' as you call it, then he might have a better chance of escaping?" Instead of ruffling his beard, Cam now was massaging his temples, as if that would help him understand. "So why don't you help him, then?"

I sighed; a bit of a compromise with Cam, I guess. "I've thought about it, but it would probably be better for me to just wait it out and watch him fail. Besides, escaping with him would carry a lot of dead weight, and the security guard who works the outer gate of the orphanage would have better luck catching one of two instead of a solo person."

Cam nodded slightly, as though he agreed. "Makes sense, but it would always be better to have someone there to support you in a time of need. You never know if you are going to need someone's help."

I rolled my eyes. "Always the one to place more faith in others, I see."

Cam let out a bellowing laugh. "Well, I rely on you to bring me food." He rubbed the outside of his jacket and slid his other hand under his shirt to massage his belly. "Speaking of: what amazing food did they serve today for lunch? And more importantly, did you happen to slide some leftovers out the door?"

I sighed and looked under the wooden bench I was sitting on. I reached for my small brown backpack, unzipped the main compartment, and reached inside. I turned my head back toward Cam while feeling around inside; Cam was staring at me like a hungry puppy.

"Cam, you're drooling . . . again," I said, snickering. I pulled out a piece of bread that I was sure was going stale and a ziplock bag containing some meatloaf with ketchup covering.

"Do you want this, Cam?" I asked as I swung both the bread and the ziplock bag side to side and watched Cam's eyes follow every movement.

"Sam, don't be a dick!" Cam said as he tried fitting his hand through the diamond-shaped holes in the fence.

"Whoa! Language, young man!" I said as I watched Cam continue to try to grab the food dangling from my hand.

"You know what, Sam? Fine! If you are going to be mean, then I'm leaving and heading back toward The Split. Maybe the nice folks there will share with me, or probably not—since 'us people' aren't too keen on sharing." Cam brushed the dirt off his coat, reached down, threw his bag onto his back, and turned to walk away.

"Aww, come on! Don't be such a baby!" I said as Cam continued walking. "Fine!" I said, sighing. I pushed the food through the fence.

The second the food hit the ground, I could physically see Cam's ears and entire face perk up. He immediately whipped his head around and took a few hasty steps toward the fallen meal. He didn't even take a moment to unlock the bag. He placed part of the bag in his teeth, ripped it off, and then I watched in horror—it was like a beast devouring his prey. Once the meatloaf was gone, he stuffed the whole piece of bread inside his mouth, took two bites, and then swallowed whole. He took a few moments to collect his thoughts, wipe his face, and then turned back toward me.

"What's the matter? You ain't never seen a grown man eat before? Is it because I'm black?" Cam said, chuckling to himself and then wiping his face one more time to ensure no crumbs went to waste.

"It is a marvel watching you eat," I said, laughing. "Also: why you always pulling the black card up? You do one thing I think is weird and all of a sudden I'm the perpetrator!"

Cam licked his fingers to make sure he had gotten all the ketchup off his hands. I watched as he next took a lone crumb from his beard and placed it in his mouth. "I'm just giving you a hard time because you were teasing me. You big jerk!" Cam said as he continued to survey his dense beard for crumb scraps.

"Anyway, I want to hear more about this Jekyll kid," he said. "It sounds like his failure might be your beginning. Why not help him out in his escape, and you can see the pitfalls—or ins and outs—of getting out." Cam was now extra excited because he found a spare chunk of meatloaf on his jacket. He gulped it down and smiled at me.

"Gross," I said, sighing. I slowly shook my head back and forth. "I'm just not up for it is all. I don't see the point."

"You don't see the point in a lot of things nowadays. Ever since I met you it's nothing this, nothing that. You need some substance, some soul," Cam said as he hummed the last part of "soul" and raised his hands in the air to signify some sort of glory above.

"Yeah, I'll think about it. There's not a whole lot of soul to be had." I could feel the tiredness of this conversation start to seep into my face.

"Talk to Jekyll. Tell him you'll help, even if it means just keeping an eye out. It will give you something to do. Something to keep your mind off of . . . what happened," Cam said as he looked away to avoid making eye contact with me. He knew it best not to look directly at me since he had mentioned the most painful thing in my life.

"I'll see," I said as I slowly lifted myself off the bench, brushed myself off, grabbed my small bag, and started walking toward the building.

"Sam, one last thing."

I slowed my step and turned back to face him. "What, Cam? I have to go."

"He can't take anything from you anymore, so you might as well let him go and live life to the fullest," Cam said, this time looking right at me, as grasped the fence.

I stared back. Took a deep breath and swallowed. "You're wrong. He still has everything to take."

I turned my back and walked toward the building. "He still has everything to take," I whispered to myself, again and again, as I kept walking.

ELEVEN

NEBULOUS IGNORANCE

The sound of the cardiac monitor murmurs in the background. *Beep, beep, beep,* followed by a subtle pause and then a melodic recourse, over and over. I slowly open my eyes. My throat feels dry as I force down a painful swallow of saliva. My eyes automatically shutter themselves from the light of the room; I slowly open them in slits and glance back and forth to survey my surroundings. The curtain into the room is closed.

I lift my right hand but am met by resistance. I try lifting my left hand—more resistance. I groggily lift my head and peer down my body. I'm covered in a surgery gown and a small inkjet of blood ranges from the right side of my chest to the crevice in my bicep. I blink a couple of times to try to further accommodate my eyes to light. They feel heavy, like they want to collapse. I feel tired—so tired. I feel weak. I try lifting my arms another time, and they only lift about a foot off the bed. I look at both arms and am met by a small gleam of light reflecting off a leather strap with metal. I try lifting my arms with more force, but the effect is negligible. I start to scream out—but there is no acoustic presence. I try again—no sound. I try swallowing once again but am only met by a dry mouth gasping for fluid. I shake my arms again and the clank of metal bangs against the metal arms of the bed.

I look around the room once more—not a soul can hear me. I try to sit up but am met by a howl of pain arising from my back.

I take a deep breath and swallow. I can feel saliva coating my throat, finally giving me enough fluidity to speak. "Hello?" I crackle. "Hello . . . is anyone there?" The room remains silent all but for the subtle murmur of the cardiac monitor. I swallow again. This time I force down a large breath of air.

"Hello!" I scream with as much force as I can.

The sound of a chair rolling around outside the curtain can be heard. "Hold on one second." The voice muffles itself around the curtain. Then a few shortened footsteps and the curtain is pulled back.

"Clara?" I say, astonished. "Where am I? Where's Cam? Everything hurts. Can you take these damn cuffs off my arms so I can at least try to sit up?" I yank my arms away from the metal bed arms only to be met by a loud clanks. Clara walks to my bed and places her hand on my leg.

"Do you not remember what happened earlier?"

I shook my head violently. "What're you talking about?" I crackled. "Where is Cam? Do you know where he is? Is he here in the hospital?" I stare at her intently, flexing both my arms, hoping to get away from the cuffs.

She moves her hand up and down on my leg to try to calm me down. "Sam, I need to explain a couple of things to you. But I need you to remain calm, and if you do, I promise I will take these cuffs off of you." A trio of nurses walk by and peer around the curtain into the room. I can sense their curiosity.

Clara lifts her hand off my leg, walks to the other side of the room, turns on the lights, and closes the curtain. I take a deep breath and slowly close and open my eyes in an attempt to show I am consciously calming down. Clara walks over to the left side of the bed, releases the restraint, and then moves to the other side of the room and does the same.

I raise my right hand to my face and feel alongside the cut, now covered by gauze and tape. Clara turns her head back to me, and she is grabbing a chair. "Hey, don't touch that! Do you want it to get infected?" She slaps my hand down to the bed. I sit there stunned and just staring at her curiously. She pulls the chair up to the bed and reaches for my hand. She cups both her hands around mine and allows her wrists to rest on the bed under the metal bed arms.

"Clara, where am I? Where is Cam? Why does everything hurt? What're you doing here, too?" I can feel my heart pounding at the release of each question.

Clara sighs for a moment and then takes a deep breath. "Sam, I'm going to start with the simple answers and work my way up to the more complex ones. Does that make sense?"

I nod.

"Starting with where are you. You are currently at St. Francis Hospital in the observatory wing. A report came in about a young man who had major lacerations on his face and was screaming out for help in an alleyway downtown near Main Street. An ambulance picked you up and transported you here. We attempted to stitch up the cuts on your forehead and cheek, but you had a severe outburst and ended up tearing the cuts again. We had to sedate you. After sedating you, we restrained you in hopes of preventing another outburst. We moved you to the observation wing because we needed the beds for further patients." She paused. "Does any of this sound familiar?"

I shake my head in response as I stare deeply into her eyes. "What outburst? What are you talking about?" I have nothing but confusion.

"You violently sat up in bed, screaming, 'Where's Cam?' And you wouldn't say anything else. You had a fervor about you like you were going to rip the frame from the bed. It took four nurses and a doctor to restrain you. Does anything of this jog your memory?"

I look directly at her and can feel my heart tremble under the weight of my feelings. "Clara?"

I can see . . . tears welling up in her eyes. A subtle trickle stretches down from her right eye, but she is quick to wipe it away. "Sam, do you remember the first night I met you?"

I shake my head in response and flex my forearms.

She clenches my hand tightly and briefly looks down and then back up at me. "Sam, the first night I met you, it looked as though something had broken inside of you. It was my job to help stop the bleeding in your right arm." Clara lowers her gaze to my right fore-arm, and I follow. The scar is purple, red, and raised from the base of my skin. "I kept asking you questions, but there were no answers. It looked as though no one was home inside your eyes. You had no look of disgust, of anger, of torment—it looked as though you were in a coma. All your vitals read normal. Now, Sam, when you came in yes-terday, that look was gone. The look in your eyes was different—like pain had come at a cost. Sam, when you came into the ER, we noticed something while you were unconscious. We performed a physical and found bruising patterns . . . indicative of abuse, or . . . " She swallows harshly and exhales forcefully.

"I . . . " I freeze as I try to bring some words to the surface.

"Sam, were you molested?"

I shake my head so quickly that I can feel the pain of the cut on my cheek scream at me to slow down and not cause so much tension. "Where's Cam? He can tell you everything. I need Cam here!"

Clara looks puzzled. "Who is Cam? You keep repeating his name, but I have never heard of him before. Or seen him. So, who's Cam?"

I clench her hand with force.

"Ahh! Sam, stop. You're hurting me!"

She rips her hand away and pulls her arm close to herself. "Who is Cam?" She is getting more insistent.

"Cam was there on the roof! When I saw him, I thought he was dead, but no one will tell me what's going on! Just fucking tell me where Cam is! He wasn't there when I tried to climb down in the morning. Just tell me where Cam is!" I scream, and tears are bursting from my eyes. At the same time, my throat feels like it is going to col-lapse under the weight of itself.

"Sam, calm down." Clara is getting more insistent. "I can't help you if you keep losing it every time like this."

I bury my face in my sheets. "So much pain. There's so much pain," I scream out, though it's muffled. The world around me feels like it's going to collapse.

The curtain on the far side of the room rips open. A voice: "Is everything alright in here, Clara?"

"Yeah, everything's fine," Clara answers. "We just need a moment to ourselves." Clara takes a breath, places her hand on top of my head, and starts massaging.

The voice mumbles something and the curtain closes.

"I just want everything back the way it was. I just want to be alone with *her—with my MOM*! No one else!" I scream out, tears cascading down my face and gargling my outcry.

Clara says nothing. She sits in silence and continues to massage my head.

"It hurts so much!" I cry out.

"Everything is alright, Sam," Clara says as she grabs my right arm and begins moving her fingers up and down.

I continue to cry until there is nothing left. Tear by tear, they roll off my face and meet the soft blanket below. My cheek and forehead are cracking from the absorbed salt.

"I'm so sorry, Sam, for everything that has happened to you," Clara says as she reaches across the bed, grabs my arm, and slowly strokes it up and down alongside the burn.

"I . . . I . . . I . . . " I try to speak but whatever comes out is muffled by tears and what is probably slight hyperventilation.

"Sam, I know this is hard for you, but I need you to tell me how you ended up in that alley," Clara says as she continues to stroke my arm bit by bit.

I slowly lift my head from the blanket. Tears streaming down my face, eyes watery and runny. I slowly lift myself up and sit higher on my bed for a few minutes. I look over to Clara and her concerned face. I pull the covers slowly off my legs and my body, exposing my skin to the air of the room. I place both hands on the bed railing and try to heave myself over.

"Sam, what are you doing?" Clara's voice turns sharp as she tries to grab me.

I hobble over the metal railings and place both my feet on the floor. It feels cold and unwelcoming. Clara is pleading "Sam, get back into bed! You're in no condition to be walking around!"

I turn to Clara, tears still streaming down my face. I open my mouth and the influx of air and mixture of salt finds a way to seep into the cut on my cheek. "Ahh!" I mutter, wincing, as I place my hand under my jaw to aid in clamping it.

"Sam, stop! You need to get back in bed and rest. You are not well enough to be walking around. For all we know, you could have a severe concussion from hitting your head on the asphalt in the alley!" Clara places her hand on my shoulder in an effort to lead me back to bed.

I shrug it off and look over at her; my tears are slowing a bit, replaced by the determination to move. With my hand clamped to the underside of my jaw, I look her in the eyes. "You're not her. I need to find Cam. Nothing is going to stop me from walking out of this ER." I reach across my body and looked down to see my arm tethered to an IV. I unclamp my arm from under my jaw and cringe as my cheek howls in pain.

"Sam, stop! Please! I'm going to have to call security if you have another outburst!"

I briefly look at her and see more tears welling in her eyes. "Sam, please. I don't want to see you in any more pain. Please, just get back into the bed. I'll grab you something to eat from the cafeteria. You have to be exhausted and hungry. Please, get back into the bed." She is pleading.

I reach down, remove the bandage from my arm, and slowly remove the inserted needle. I cringe as I pull it out. The moment the needle exits, blood starts pooling on top of my skin and rushing down the side of my forearm.

"Sam!" Clara yells.

I grab a loose piece of surgical gown and press it hard into my arm while clamping my jaw with the other. I slowly start limping toward the curtain.

"Sam, stop!" Clara yells. When I open the curtain to the ER floor, I am met by near silence; multiple nurses are staring at me. All typing has stopped, and even the patients on the other side of the room talking to nurses are looking at me.

"Even if you leave, where will you go?" Clara demands. "You have no clothes with you! The ones you were wearing when you came in here are muddied, bloody, and torn beyond repair! You have nothing else, no backpack, no phone, no money. What are you going to do?

Roam around downtown waiting to die? Even if you find a way to get food, money, clothes, and a place to sleep, that cut will get infected and you could lose your jaw. Get back in bed and we'll talk this out! Please. I am begging you!"

I turn back to Clara. One hand clamps my jaw, the other applies pressure to the IV site. Tears are streaming down Clara's horror stricken face.

I try to fight back the pain and anguish of everything around me. "I have to find Cam. If I don't find him, then I don't know what I will do. He is the only reason why I'm still alive . . . and he might be dead! I need to help him. I can't stay in here while he might be out there hurting!" Tears once again stream down my face. My legs feel weak; I crumble to my knees. . . .

. . . When I woke up at that morning on the roof, everything hurt. Yes, my body hurt; I woke up in my own blood, destroyed, alien to myself. But the thought of Cam being dead . . . while physical pain is bearable, the loss of a loved one lingers. It vibrates down to your core—rattles your bones, deflates your lungs. Everything seems to cloud together in a fog. I have already experienced the feeling of suffocating in that fog—twice—so . . . never again! The only thing that can offer me salvation is the thought that Cam is still alive. He wasn't there when I woke up. This means he could still be alive, and if that is the case, I need to find him.

I look around the ER room and everyone—I mean, everyone—is staring at me. I slowly turn my sulking eyes back to Clara, who is five feet away, watching to see what I will do.

"You don't understand. I need him," I tell her. I let go of the IV site and blood starts to pool and drain down the subtle contour of the veins on my arm. I unclench my jaw and can feel air rush into my mouth and nip at the inside of the cut.

"I have to leave. Even if you try to stop me, I need to leave."

Clara brushes her eyes with her scrubs and takes a brief step toward me.

"Stop!" I say as I slowly lift my arm and push myself off the ground and back onto my feet. My body feels heavy and blood is beginning to streamline off my finger and drop onto the linoleum floor. I slow limp my way to the square desk nursing station of the observatory floor. "Where is the exit?" I ask the first nurse I make eye contact with, muttering as I raise my hand to place it under my jaw again.

The nurse slowly lifts her arm and points back toward the curtain enclosure where Clara is standing. "Sir, you should get back in bed."

I shake my head and stumble down the desk to another nurse, sitting adjacent to the first. "Sir . . . " I start. I cough and can feel my skin trying to hold itself together despite a rigorous exhale of air. "Sir, where is the exit?" I ask.

Again, the nurse points back to the room with Clara. "Sir, please, go back to your room. You're better off that way."

I sneer at him and turn to survey the room. "Where the fuck is the exit!" I scream out in pain and anguish. The nurse I had just talked to prior sighs heavily. "One moment, sir."

The nurse gets up from his chair and disappears down the hallway. A few moments pass, and he returns accompanied by another woman. "This is Kelly. She is the charge nurse on duty." The nurse turns and looks to Kelly briefly. "Kelly, this young man wants to leave 'AMA.'"

Kelly turns quickly to look at me. Clara has now appeared from the room located directly behind me. "Sir, do you understand that you are seeking to leave against medical advice or 'AMA' as we call it."

I scowl at her. "Yes, I want to leave."

"Alright, one moment sir." Kelly retreats behind the desk and searches for piece of paper. She quickly pulls it out of a file and places it on the front desk along with a pen. "Alright, you need to sign here. Just so you fully understand, the hospital is not responsible for your situation once you leave. Once again, we recommend that you remain here and finish receiving care."

I say nothing and quickly sign the paper with my left hand while clenching my jaw with the other.

The room stays silent besides the subtle murmur of cardiac monitors and various other monitoring devices.

Kelly grabs the paper, pushes it into a folder, and then disappears back down the hallway. I look to the left and then quickly to the right. "How the hell do I get out of here!" I scream.

"It's over there!"

A voice rings out from the opposite side of the room. I turn my head to meet the voice, and a little boy is standing alongside his family, grasping his mother's hand and holding a small doll dangling about an inch above the floor. I survey the area and find the general direction the boy is pointing. I look back at the boy and his mom is scolding him, in a hushed tone, for having spoken. The mother briefly looks up from her son and immediately locks eyes with me. I catch her eyes for a moment, but then turn my body away and start stumbling toward the exit. Step by step, I trudge through the ER—as everyone watches.

Blood is now dripping from my arm onto my leg; each drop seems to cascade down my dry and frail legs. Step by step, my path can be seen. I walk toward the exit, place my feet on the black strip, and the automatic door opens. A burst of warm air presses against my surgical gown. I walk a couple of steps outside, and a voice rings out behind me.

"Sam, if you insist on leaving, at least give me a minute to give you a couple of things!" I turn my head. Clara is standing in the doorway with a plastic bag filled with various objects that I can't make out. "If you are that adamant about leaving, take this with you and let me tape your cut shut so it doesn't get infected. I am begging you: please let me help."

I shake my head again and turn back toward the outside, and night. I take a step forward and can feel my arm being wrenched.

"Sam, listen to me! You may not want my help, but if you leave here without any kind of help—medical or anything else—you will not last more than a day. You have no clothing, no food, no money, and no shelter. At least take this with you and let me bandage your arm quickly before you set out."

I stare down into the bag. It has a pair of black sweatpants, a T-shirt, some shoes, and other clothing.

"Let me see your arm," Clara says as she reaches for my right arm and pulls it to extension. I instinctively place my left hand under my jaw to help ease the pain.

She drops the bag to the ground, laces my arm with bandages, and then seals it in with a plastic layer of bandaging.

She looks up at me and smiles. "At least this way, you won't get an infection!"

"Thank you," I murmur under my breath.

She smiles for a moment. "Sweetheart, I may not understand exactly what you are setting out to do, but there is no way I can let you go out into the city in the condition you are in now."

Tears begin to well in my eyes. A single tear rolls down my face, drops off my chin, and lands on Clara's hand as she finishes bandaging. She looks up at my face, swollen by emotion, and lifts both her hands up to it. With both hands pressed against the underside of my face, she wipes the tears away with her thumbs. "Sweetheart, I don't know what you are doing or who you are looking for, but I want you to know something." Clara brushes a shallow tear away from the corner of her eye. "If you ever need something, I want you to come right back here and get ahold of me. I will always be here for you."

She looks to the ground and lifts the bag, then thrusts it at me. "It's not much, but there's two pairs of clothes in here from people . . . who no longer need them. I also put a little money in there to help you out. I'm so sorry for everything, sweetheart." Clara continues brushing the tears streaming down my face, bends my chin down, and gives me a kiss on the forehead.

"Good luck, Sam," she says as she turns back to the ER with a couple of weak steps. I watch as she walks away, still brushing her face with her sleeves. She turns the corner and disappears.

I look down into carefully tied bag and slowly open it to reveal its contents. A small wad of money falls to the ground. I bend over to pick it up. It's one hundred dollars in the form of five twenty-dollar bills. I shove it back in the bag and search deeper. A couple of shirts, a sweatshirt, some socks, and some shoes. Inside the bag is a smaller bag with a few Ibuprofen.

I close it all up and look around. It is the dead of night and outside the ER everything is quiet. I survey my surroundings; there is little but a few lights and the sound of a few crickets. The air is warm and keeps pulling and pushing at my surgical gown. Outside the ER is a simple layout. Two brick pillars rise to hold the large metal flat ceiling that extends into the parking lot. The ER entrance loops around in a circular fashion for easy ambulance access. I slowly trudge to one of the brick pillars and drop the bag. I reach inside and pull out a pair of baggy, black, stained sweatpants and tug them over the underpart of my surgical gown. Once covering my lower half, I remove the surgical gown, reach into the bag, and pull out a white T-shirt; it has a Corona logo on the front. I slowly pull it over my face and arms to avoid tearing the bandaging. I reach into the bag and pull out shoes and a pair of black socks. I find a way to tug them on.

I reach down and tie up the bag and remaining loose ends around my left hand to ensure it isn't torn away or stolen. I walk on, out into the darkness of the night, heading toward the nearest streetlight. "I need to find Cam . . . " I mutter to myself. I slowly leave the ER behind me.

"Where would Cam go if he got away from that . . . monster?" I grit my teeth and can feel the cut on my cheek howl from the tightening of the muscles in my face.

"I'm going to make that asshole pay for what he did to Cam," I say to myself as I reach my hands in my pocket. I clutch my legs and sigh as I take a step forward.

TWELVE

HOMECOMING

Let me pose a question. When the world collapses on your shoulders, what do you do? Go home? Find somewhere safe and warm, like your bed? Eat comfort food?

What if none of these amenities are available and you're alone? What if the only thing that comforts the pain of the world is the marginal amount of light flickering in the distance? The light emanating from a city of people living together, miles and miles away from you. Now do you see what it really is? It's the people. But many of those people have driven themselves to a lonely hell; they've become homogenized by the silence and vacant spaces. And if you thought there would be some sort of comfort in being alone together, there isn't. Some say silence is golden, but I don't agree. I've felt its icy claws wrap around me, shouting at me, yelling to make sure I don't forget that I am truly *alone*. And loneliness is a different kind of pain. It's emotional, dehumanizing. It eats you up from the inside out, demanding your suffering—with no release. It is so agonizing that it robs you and leaves you with nothing left to feel.

"I am lonely," I whisper to myself. I shudder. I feel more tears welling up. "I want to be home. I want to be warm." Tears press against the surface of my eyes and slowly push their way past my so-very-tired eyelids. "I just don't want to be alone," I say to no one but myself. Tears are now gushing down my face and slowly dripping toward the ground. "I can't do this anymore! I need to find Cam!" I pause; then a different thought. "I wish she was still here with me." An anaerobic gasp from too much crying swells within my lungs. I look toward the stars. The tears in my eyes mitigate the light from the city. But all I can see is the faint glimpse of one star. All others are blocked by air and light pollution.

I look back at the ground and continue trudging toward the fixed streetlights. Every three hundred feet or so, a neon orange streetlight punches a hole in the darkness of the street. There is about twenty feet of "safe haven," and then the dark swallows the light back up. I lift my head and continue to press the underside of my jaw shut. "This Advil isn't doing anything!" I scream in a sudden outburst. There is nothing. Nothing but the silent echo howling back at me from the street. "How many do I have to take to make the pain go away!" I ask myself. I've already swallowed twelve pills whole with no water. I can make out the slight piece of a pill nestled in the back of my throat, but I'm too weak to jiggle it free through coughing or digging it out with my hand. Besides, any excess movement to my jaw is something I clearly want to avoid.

Still trudging, I approach the next streetlight. A bus stop with a small shelter to help people avoid the rain is a mere ten feet away. The light shimmering down from the stop looks as though it is clinging to the edge of the shelter. Pleading that it not move farther into the darkness. Step by step, I can feel the weight of my body becoming unbearable. The muscle in my arm aches from the IV being ripped out. My jaw wants to scream with each small inhale—so much so that I try to stop breathing through my mouth entirely. Step by step, heart-beat after heartbeat, I am done with this day. I need to sleep. I need the pain to go away.

I approach the edge of the bus stop and warily peer inside, around the corner and into partial darkness. No one. I feel my heart skip a beat, but I write it off as pain. I drag myself inside the little shelter and sit on the side closest to the light. The light seems to form tendrils—each tendril trying to work its way into the enclosed space, but only specks of light, it seems, are strong enough to work their way in.

I toss the plastic bag with the money, Advil, and clothes on the ground. I lean my head against the side of the stop and peer up at the light a final time. I flex the muscles in my face in the hope of drawing a slight smile, but the pain far exceeds that hope. I slowly close my eyes. Actually, it's more like my eyes close on me. They are sick of the world, sick of the pain—they just want it to end. They want peace. Right now, they just want a dream.

THIRTEEN

ROCK BOTTOM

"Sam!" A voice screams out from inside my head. "Sam!"

"What! What could you possibly want? Leave me alone!" I force out my own scream, one of agony and despair.

"Wake! You need to wake!"

The pain is immense. The sound is daunting. Bit by bit, I can feel my senses trickling back into my body. My eyes slowly roll to the front from the back of my head. I let out a large exhale of pain.

Crshh . . . Crshh.

I sit in a stupor; the sound keeps invading my ears.

Crshh . . . Crshh.

"Ahh, my head!" I say to no one. "What the hell is that sound?"

Crshh . . . Crshh.

It sounds like a plastic bag rustling back and forth.

My eyes shoot open and I glance downward, in the general direction of where I had thrown the bag. And then . . . an influx of light from the sun outside. It tortures my eyes as they seek to frantically adjust.

"No, no, no!" I blurt out. "Please, just give me one fucking break!

101

It's all I need!"

The sound is my plastic bag, floating back and forth on the inside of the bus stop. Rustling with each change in the wind and scraping the sides of metal plating on the inside edges of the stop. But . . . it is apparently empty.

"Fuck! The money is gone! The clothes are gone! The medicine is gone!" I frantically sit up and scour the inside of the bus stop. "Where is it? Where is it?" *Maybe it fell out of the bag or maybe I put some in my pocket.* I am trying to think quickly. I plunge my hands in my pockets. I rip the pockets outward from the sweatpants. I can feel my eyes widen as I discover I am finding . . . nothing.

What if someone around here saw the stuff in my bag being taken? It's the only thought I have. I tighten my legs and push myself to stand up. Uhh . . . nothing. I try again, exhorting force on my legs to make them support my weight.

Come on, stupid body! I scream in my head. *Let me up!* I cock my arms to the side and swing as hard as I can. With each pulse of electricity, I can feel my legs slowly starting to wake. Bit by bit, I move them into position. I pull myself toward the bus stop opening and swing my head side to side in hopes of finding someone. As I look to the left, something catches my eye. A small black shape is slowly getting smaller. I squint to see more clearly. A small woman with a walker—tennis balls underneath, for support—is heading in the direction of the hospital.

"Hey! Hey you!" I blurt out.

Nothing changes.

"Hey, lady! Stop!"

The woman slowly comes to a stop and turns her head. She still seems a great distance away.

I pull myself around the corner of the bus stop door and sprint in her direction. The lady turns back. She's moving very slow, but begins to speed up as I get closer.

"Stop," I blurt out. "I need to talk to you!"

As I close the distance between us, she turns her walker and locks eyes with me. "Stay away from me, you crazy homeless boy! Get back. I have mace," she roars in self-defense.

Her eyes are locked on me; she is tracing any small movement I make. I scan up and down and see a black bag dangling from her walker. I take a small step toward her.

"I mean it, kid. Back off or you're going to get it!" she says as the left upper side of her lip rises to a snarl.

"You took my money, didn't you, you crazy old hag?" I say through gritted teeth.

"I didn't take anything from you. Now leave me alone or I am going to call the cops."

"Yeah, we'll see about that." *She probably has my money and clothes in that black bag.* The thought echoes in my head.

I lift my feet and close more distance between me and her. "Give me the bag, you hag!" I rip the bag from the walker and begin to look inside.

"There's no . . . " I'm beginning to speak when the right side of my face feels as though it has been lit on fire. "*Ahh!!*" I scream in pain. The cut on the right side of my face is searing with agony. Each individual nerve feels as though it is pulling away from my face in an attempt to escape. My legs feel weak from the pain and I collapse on the grass next to the sidewalk the old woman is standing on. "*Ahh!!* My face. My face!*" The pain from my cut slowly starts leeching toward other parts of my face. My eyes, my nostril. Everything is on fire. "What did you do?" I scream in the general direction of the woman.

"I told you to leave me alone or you were going to get pepper-sprayed! Serves you right!" says the woman. Now just a black blob, she quickly turns and continues down the sidewalk.

I am still screaming as waves of pain oscillate between my eyes, cut, and the nostrils on my face. I turn my face toward the grass. Something wet caresses my face ever so slightly even as my face feels as though it is being torn to pieces. The dew from the grass is cold, but there is enough to make the pain begin to stop. I clutch at the grass and begin ripping parts of it away. Bit by bit, I rub the dew-soaked grass all over my face. The pain slowly begins to dissipate. Grass mound by grass mound, I cover my face with the stuff.

I lay there with my legs extended on the grass—face down.

This is it. I am going to die here. My jaw and my arm and my soul are going to fall out of my body and rot on the pavement. But . . . *I am OK with this. I am OK with this. At least, the pain will subside and I will finally get to be with my mom. Everything will be great. I will get a warm bed in Heaven—and the food . . . Damn, the food will be amazing. I can almost taste it now. It will be 100 percent better than that crappy Salisbury steak Cam loves so much.* I actually start to giggle. But as each second passes, the pain seeps in and the giggles quickly die away. One by one, I can feel the nerves inside my mouth adjacent to the cut scream in agony. I press my hand against my jaw and clamp it shut.

"I need to find Cam." I say this out loud as I slowly push myself off the ground with my other arm. I push my aching joints to an erect position and start to brush myself off. Grass covers my entire shirt and pants. "Great. As if the garbage I'm wearing now doesn't look crappy enough," I say, managing at least a measure of sarcasm.

I look toward the sky and the sun is now gleaming down. It looks as though it is just past 7 A.M. The sun has already pushed past the mountains in the distance. I look toward the financial district downtown. Sunlight is radiating off the tall glass skyscrapers, reflecting in all directions.

Wow, it almost looks peaceful down there. And I know that even though that piece of shit is lurking the streets somewhere down there, I need to find Cam.

I guess this is as low as a person can get. I turn my body away from the direction of the hospital and slowly start pacing toward the downtown district. I need to go to The Split. I need to know if Cam is still alive somewhere.

FOURTEEN

BETTY AT THE SPLIT

It's been about two hours since I departed from the grassy bed I had, for a brief time, called my resting place. Bit by bit, I trudge onward. Each step is accompanied by a forced exhale and a howl of pain shooting from my bicep and screaming out of my cut. The view of The Split is now, finally, coming into view. If Cam is going to be somewhere, he will be at The Split. Also, most of The Split's "patrons" will probably still be lingering, and I might be able to get some information; it's too early for the lunch rush toward the East Hills shelter.

As I travel the sidewalk, out of the corner of my eyes I see people driving by. Each car seems to bring a different stare. A stare of pity. One of relief. A stare of disbelief. And the eventual outburst of comedy. "Hey, dipshit! Nice clothes. Where'd you get them? The garbage dump is back the way you came." Within a few seconds the cars pass and a new onslaught of comments is directed my way. As I approach the sidewalk to enter the first underpass of The Split, I stop for the hectic traffic. I watch as the red crossing lights count down to zero; it's hypnotic. "I'm exhausted," I let out in a whisper; I can feel my head actually nodding up and down with each change of the seconds. I glimpse down from the traffic light for a moment and am met by the eyes of a little girl. She's in a car with her father. The window is slightly open.

"Hey Daddy. What's wrong with that boy's clothes?" I can hear her question.

The large man sitting next to the little girl in the front seat turns his head and slowly lifts his sunglasses. "Oh, sweetheart, it's just a homeless boy. There is nothing to be worried about." The man lowers his glasses and turns back to facing the stoplight.

The little girl quickly removes her face from the window and whips her head toward her father. "Well, shouldn't we give him something? Like some money or some food or some clothes?" She says it loudly, with a child's passion.

The father continues to look straight ahead. "Sweetie, he probably has a mental deficiency, or he will probably just go blow it on alcohol or something bad. We should just let him be. He will find his way."

The girl turns back to me and stares. I look into her deep blue eyes and can feel a pit in my throat growing larger and larger.

I stand up straight—well, as straight as I can. I grimace at the girl. Then I direct my eyes right at the dad.

"Hey, dipshit!" I let out in a strong, concerted tone.

The girl looks shocked and looks to her father. He removes his glasses and stares in my direction—his look is sullen. I am, somehow, more than ready for him with my words.

"I am by no means retarded," I say, plenty loud for him to hear. "I am not mentally deficient. And yeah, I could use your help a little. This is all I have right now. Nothing. I am wearing basically garbage with grass stains all over me from head to toe. I am starving. I am exhausted, and you have no idea what kind of day, what kind of week, or as a matter of a fact, what kind of life I have had!"

People from cars all around are now looking in my direction. One by one, their windows slowly fall; they want to hear what all this commotion is. I continue to stare at the dad. Words seem to fill up inside of me. I am far from done.

"You have no fucking idea who I am. What I have done. And the worst part, besides the fact that you made multiple guesses on my behalf, is that you taught your daughter that people that look like us or walk like us or have any similar mannerisms as us are all trash. We are something to be ignored. Something to be wiped under the rug because you know what we are." I can feel my voice rising with each word. Tears are starting to well up, once again, in my eyes.

"We are you at your worst," I tell him, finishing my speech.

I look across the sea of cars. I notice that all the adjacent traffic lights have finally turned green. I turn my head quickly back to the father; he is snarling at me. His face looks tense; all his face muscles seem taut.

I look again at his daughter. Her face is now somehow different. A look of amazement, even stupor. The poor girl isn't at all sure what she is witnessing.

"Hey!" screams the father my way. "Leave her out of this, asshole! Why don't you take your pills or whatever you forgot to take today and crawl back into that dirty hole you crawled out of? Leave us out of it!" He jerks his head forward and immediately raises his lowered window. As he pulls away, into the intersection and beyond, the little girl presses her face against the glass. I watch as her eyes stay locked on me as her father drives on.

The remaining cars also slowly begin to pull forward. I grit my teeth and can feel all the muscles in my face pulsate with adrenaline and fear. The cut in my face, now on fire, is matched by the pain and tightness radiating across my face. "I just want to fucking find Cam!" I let out in a large, anguished exhale.

When the walking light flickers across the street, I lower myself from the curb, a task that feels much harder than usual, and continue on my way to The Split. This is when I hear the female voice.

"Wow, Mr. Samuel. Quite the performance we are putting on today. Was that for them? Or was that for you? Did you run out of drugs, sweetheart?"

I look up, about halfway across the crosswalk, and there is Betty standing, smiling. Betty is an interesting character. She always wears ragged green clothes and black pants along with a black belt positioned in a diagonal across her hips. She has semi-short silver hair and a green camouflage bandanna. Her smile is irradiant; this despite the fact she only has three teeth, and the two outer ones are partially rotted on either side of her one larger front tooth.

I continue walking toward her, but in silence. Everything hurts. My face still feels as though it wants to scream out—it just doesn't want to have to use my voice. I trudge by Betty and keep my gaze fixed on the ground.

"Kiddo, what's wrong?" Betty asks as she places her hand on my shoulder from behind and gives a slight pull in hopes of turning me around. I just stare at the ground. "Nothing," she says, answering her own question, in a sarcastic tone as she walks around my body from back to front. She reaches for my chin, still tucked toward my chest, and slowly raises it so she can look at my face. My eyes finally lock with hers. The look in her eyes is almost indescribable. I want to cry because of that look, but I have no emotion left to do so. I'm just exhausted. Crying uses energy, and I no longer have any.

"Oh, kiddo," she says as she turns my head to the side to get a better look at the cut. "What happened?"

"I don't want to talk about it," I say quietly.

"And what happened to your clothes? It looks like these were pulled out of the bottom of the river and then a car ran over them."

I let out a large, slow exhale and just stare over her shoulder at The Split.

"I don't want to talk about it," I repeat. This time my voice is lower, more angered.

She pulls my chin up so she can look into my eyes. "I'm sorry, sweetie, but here. I have something that can take away the pain." She smiles softly as she removes her large black backpack and lowers it to the ground. She reaches into the bag and grimaces. "Damn it! Where is it? I know I always have at least one on me." She stops digging for a moment and looks up at me. "Helps you through those oh-so-cold nights." She giggles as she returns to her bag and keeps digging. Betty is grimacing. She reaches farther down into her pack—the pack opening is now close to her shoulder.

Almost as fast as I can blink, a smile lights up her face. "Here we go!" she says in what sounds like ecstasy. She tugs at something, but her backpack seems as though it has a mind of its own and wants to fight her tug. Almost as if it wants what she does as much as she does. "Just one more big pull!" Betty yells.

I look at her face and all the veins above her forehead are pressed against the surface of her skin. Her skin transitions to a rose color and then to a full-on red as she tugs with all her might.

"Got it!" she lets out in a large exhale and falls on her back. She wheezes heavily and coughs with grotesque heaves as I watch her chest lunge up and down. "All worth it!" she says as she rolls onto her side exposing a fifth of Tennessee whiskey—Jack Daniels, honey style. She extends her hand full of the fifth of whiskey right at me.

I just stare at the bottle and then back at her. Then back at the bottle and back at her.

"That will just . . . Whatever! If you don't take the first swig, I will!"

Betty leans onto her back, unscrews the cap, and proceeds to take what looks more like an inhale than a swallow of whiskey. She removes the bottle from her mouth and lets out a large exhale . . . of whiskey. "Always makes me feel better!" She turns back to me and again extends the bottle in my direction. Then, she pulls it back. "Actually, one more for the road," she says, giddily, as she smiles and pulls the bottle frantically to her face. Betty lets out a brief smile and then wraps her lips around the bottle. It's then that I hear it . . .

"You're my hero, lady! Keep on rocking!" yells a voice from behind me. I whip my body around to see two guys driving past in a red Corvette; they're grinning from ear to ear with excitement. "Take a chug for the boys!" they yell as they speed off.

I turn back to Betty to see her smiling while looking down at the ground and raising the bottle toward the cement overpass of The Split. She laughs briefly at me as she looks up. "Can't let my fans down now, can I?" She falls back to the ground again, opens wide, then proceeds to take two large swigs. With a loud "Ppppchhhh!" she lowers the bottle from her lips. She roughly places the cap back on top, screws it shut, and sends the bottle rolling in my direction. She starts laughing sporadically, followed by a grotesque cough, and then more sporadic laughing.

"I am going to be feeling . . . he-he . . . oh-so-good in a couple of minutes," she lets out with a rough chuckle.

Quickly, she pulls herself to her side and stares at me. Almost as if staring into my soul. "Now, young one . . . drink. No more pain . . . except for the first swig." She buries herself in her coat arm and lets out a big burp followed by a large cough. "It will only make you feel better," she says, smiling and exposing her lonesome teeth to the penetrating daylight seeping in from outside The Split.

I let out an indifferent shrug and reach for the bottle, rolling slightly back and forth on the uneven sidewalk cement. I pick up the bottle, remove the cap, and raise the thing to my mouth. The strong smell of alcohol rushes through my nose and penetrates each open pore it can find. I let out a large, forced exhale of disgust.

"Bottoms up, trooper!" Betty yells from the ground as she continues to stare up at the ceiling of The Split.

So here I go . . . I place the bottle against my bottom lip, take a brief inhale, and move the bottle to my upper lips. I close my lips around it. I close my eyes. I can feel the alcohol running down the back of my throat after it brushes against the sides of my cheeks and now down toward my stomach. My eyes shoot open and I rip the bottle away from my mouth. I slam the bottle to the grass and immediately reach to my mouth. I open my jaw. I can feel each nerve scream out as the whiskey presses against the inside of my mouth.

"Ow, ow, ow!!" I yell in pain. I clamp my jaw shut with both hands and then tighten my eyes, using every muscle in my face to try to override the pain.

It sounds as though Betty rolls over onto her side facing me and begins to chuckle. "The first one is . . . " she says, then a large, grotesque piece of phlegm flies out of her mouth as she forcefully coughs, then starts chuckling again. "Sorry, sweetheart. That was gross. Anyway, the first one is always the worst."

I continue to clamp my jaw shut. "It seeped into my cut!" I screech in pain. As I open my mouth, the air meeting with the cut makes it worse. Each exposed nerve cries out in a symphony of searing pain and displeasure.

Betty continues to laugh. "Well, do you know what the cure is for something that's hurting?"

I slowly shake my head. "To not have it hurt from the start?" It's the best I can come up with.

She chuckles again. She reaches for the bottle and pulls it toward her body. She raises the Jack Daniels in the air and looks me dead in the eyes. "You drink until it goes away!" She lifts the bottle to her lips and takes another large swig.

"I think I'll manage," I say as I slowly push myself off the ground and rise to my feet. "I need to go find Cam anyway. Have you seen him anywhere? Tall black man? Large beard, tattoos?"

Betty rolls onto her back once more and looks up at the ceiling of The Split. "Whatever makes you happy, sweetheart! You go on and find what makes you happy! Bughhh!!" Betty lets out a large burp and then starfishes on the pavement. She looks content. Her eyes are closed and she smiles up at The Split ceiling and the sky beyond it.

I swivel my head. "I just want to sit down and close my eyes for a minute," I whisper as I lock my eyes on a concrete bench about fifty feet away. The bench is next to one of the mural-like decorated pillars. "It will have to do for a nap," I say quietly to myself as I slowly walk that way.

I reach the bench and slowly lower myself onto it using my one spare arm. I place my shoulder against the cold, concrete pillar on my right-hand side. I can feel the steady vibrations from the highway above as each car speeds by. It's almost as if it is a lullaby. Each passing car: a sheep hurdling the fence. Each vibration: a subtle heartbeat far away.

A nice breeze hits my face and appeases the cut . . . I slowly drift into numbness. "Ahhh," I let out in a brief exhale.

Just a couple hours. Then I will figure it all out. My eyelids slowly fall. The darkness is welcoming. Away from the pain, away from the light. Just peace.

FIFTEEN

US PEOPLE

A weight suddenly presses against my shoulder. My eyes rock back and forth as I slowly try to pry them open with the energy that's left in my face.

"Ughh!" I slur out in a stupor. "What do you want?" I slowly try to adjust my eyes to the remaining light that's seeping in from outside The Split. I peer my eyes to the side. The sun is just disappearing over the hill and the light looks as though it is trying to hold itself away from the darkness peering over the opposite horizon. I close my eyes one more time and try and fight off the grogginess. "Ughh!" One more painful sound tumbles from my mouth.

"Is that anyway to greet a buddy?"

I force my eyelids open and peek in the direction of the weight on my shoulder. The weight now lifts itself from my shoulder, and a large black-coated man with green pants and tattered boots is sitting next to me on the bench.

"I've been looking for you, Sammy," the voice says in a deep tone. "I thought you might have died on that roof, but I'm glad you're still alive."

My heart pumps faster with each word the man speaks. It's starting to come to me who this is . . .

"I'm glad you're still here, Sammy."

The light from the setting sun filters in just the right way and illuminates the dark complexion of Cam's face.

My heart steadies and tears start welling in my eyes as I throw my arms around him and squeeze. Nothing feels like his embrace. The smell is so familiar, but I can never put my finger on it. For once, just once in this past week, I feel a strange sense of calm—unlike anything before. It's as though all danger has withered away by his touch.

"What happened? I thought you were dead. I knew you were dead! I saw the blood! Where did you go? Why did you leave me on the roof? Where have you *been*?!" The questions seem to gargle from my mouth in a tone of despair, at first, and then anger.

"What the fuck happened?" I yell at him. I clench my fist and slam it into the concrete pillar on my right side.

My face is wet as I explode in an emotional display of . . . tears and snot.

"Sam," he says softly. "I am glad you're OK. I know I have a lot of explaining to do, but for right now I want to make sure that you're OK."

My face goes flush and then feels as though it has been reinvigorated. It feels like it's been ages since someone actually cared for me. Since someone cared about my well-being besides myself. I bury my face in my hands. The tears are shooting past my eyes and down into the fissures created by the separation between my fingers. I can feel the tears collect there and then slowly seep through and fall to the ground.

"I'm sorry, Sammy," Cam says as he places his hand on my shoulder.

I sit there for about five minutes and just let the tears run through the seams of my hands. This isn't just catharsis. This is warranted emotional runoff. Never have I been given a break or something to encourage me to keep pressing forward. This is simple. I've been beat down until I can't trudge forward anymore. Life has tried to put me down—permanently.

I finally lift my hands and now glare at Cam. "Tell me what

happened! You left me on that roof. I almost died getting down, let alone getting raped by that asshole! You left me, Cam! You left me! You fucking left me up there!" I belt out a plethora of angry obscenities for about a minute.

Cam does nothing the whole time except stare at the ground. No emotion, no movement—just stagnation.

"Cam! Fucking answer me!" I scream.

Cam looks up at me. His face is flush and pale, his beard withered and starting to gray. "I did what I had to, to survive. I have no idea what happened. I was kicked in the face by something hard and knocked unconscious. When I woke in the morning, there was a pool of blood surrounding me, and I had a large cut in my abdomen. I looked over and saw you lying there. I tried to wake you up. I shook you as hard as I could . . . " Tears are starting to stream down Cam's face and into his beard. "Sam, you looked dead! You were lying there naked in a pool of blood. I shook you again. I shook you as many times as possible and you looked dead. Your cheek was swollen and purple from the cut and your eyes were only half open. I didn't know what to do. So I panicked and went to find help. I am sorry I left you on the roof. I am sorry I left you alone. But I did it for you. I climbed down the fire escape, dropped into the alley, and ran to find help. By the time I was able to get someone to help, you were being hauled into an ambulance and there was a trail of blood leading from the alley to the ambulance."

I continue to glare at Cam. His eyes are bloodshot from the emotion, and his face—it seems to me—is flush with embarrassment.

"And you think that I didn't walk away with scars? No one survives these streets unscathed, Sam," Cam says. Then he lifts his shirt to show fourteen stitches ranging from the lower part of his left abdomen up diagonally to the upper right side.

"Cam, I . . . "

"Also, you're not the only one, Sam. This kind of crap happens all the time on the streets. You knew this even back at that boarding school when I convinced you to leave it all behind. To be free, to control your own fate and leave your demons behind—you knew the risk. You knew it was dangerous. I told you that. I told you it was going to be hard, that you were going to have to fight to leave those demons behind. You knew the risks. You always knew the risks."

"Cam, I . . . "

"One more thing," says Cam, raising his hand and motioning for me to remain quiet. I relax my body and just look in his direction. "There seems to be something that you still don't get."

"What's that?" I quietly ask, though I am still angry.

"I watched as you screamed at those cars. We all did." At this, he motions around The Split and points at various people.

"To them, to all of them—" and he points at cars passing by. "To them, we are a reminder. They see us as something different. They don't understand that we need help, that we need someone to help us in our pursuit of something greater. To gain something more out of life. To them, we are a virus. Not of the human body, but of the human society. We represent them at their worst. We are what they don't understand. That's why when you first came out here, I never allowed you to call us homeless. Because the label defines who we are. It defines what they think we are. And it defines what you believe yourself to be."

"Cam," I interject, and he looks taken aback. "That doesn't make sense. What label? We *are* homeless! There is no beating around the bush. We have nothing. Nowhere to live. We survive by going around and begging, pleading for money if we have to. We are homeless."

Cam smiles briefly and then chuckles. "Do you know why I had you call homeless people 'Us People' from the start?"

I shake my head. I honestly do not.

"I always had you call us 'Us People' because homelessness has such a negative stigma in this b-s society we live in. What they don't understand for someone like you . . . " He points at me and then pokes me in the chest. " . . . is that for you, this is your escape to get away from the voices of society, the monsters that haunted you before. Out here—and this is not true for all, but out here—you live your life as you please. No mother, no father, no boarding school. It is you against the world. And if you ever decide that this isn't the place for you—the streets, that is—you know what the alternative is."

I shake my head, and strongly. "Wait. *What* is the alternative? What is it?"

"Let's hope you never find out, for both our sakes," Cam says, rising to his feet.

Cam brushes himself off and pats the dust from his pants.

"What happened to your backpack?" I ask.

Cam stretches his back. It looks like he's being extra careful not to stretch too far so he can avoid pain from his cut.

"I am assuming the same thing that happened to yours," he says. "Either that man took it or he threw it off the roof into a nearby alley."

Cam continues to knock the dust off his shirt and starts walking, heading down the sidewalk.

"Where are you going?" I yell. "I'm exhausted. I don't want to walk!" My jaw is in severe pain whenever I open my mouth, and I have to move quickly to clamp it shut immediately.

Cam looks in the direction of the horizon. The sun is just barely showing, and all the city lights are now gleaming in the distance.

"I don't know about you, but I don't want the same fiasco to happen as a couple nights ago," Cam says. "I want to get to the shelter before they section off the bedding for the night. Also, I am starving. But it's up to you. If you want to stay out here tonight and try to find a place to sleep, a place to eat, and some protection, be my guest. But for me, I think I'm going to try to sleep in a warm, comfortable bed tonight. And hopefully with some Salisbury steak in my belly."

I exhale deeply through my nose and slowly rise to my feet, once again clamping my arm against my jaw.

"You wouldn't happen to have any meds, would ya?" I ask Cam.

He smiles briefly and then turns to head down the sidewalk.

"If I had meds, don't you think I would be taking them instead of giving them to you?" he asks, laughing lightly. "I have absolutely nothing on me except the clothes on my back." Cam briefly turns back to face me. "I can see that he didn't leave you with even that. We need to get you some new clothes. Ones that aren't made up of leftover garbage bags. We will check the lost and found when we get to the East Hills Shelter."

"That's such a long way!" I object.

"It seems like you don't have much of a choice now, do you?" Cam says as he continues down the sidewalk and on past The Split.

I sigh and started walking after him. "Back to walking," I whisper to myself. But now that I think about it, a bed does sound extremely nice. I was in too much of a hurry to find Cam to really consider how nice that hospital bed felt.

I look toward the sky. The stars are just starting to peep through the early night sky.

SIXTEEN

ASYLUM

"Ahh, finally. There's the shelter," I say out loud, even while trying to keep my mouth opening as narrow as possible because of the pain.

"I can almost feel the warmth of the bed," Cam says. He's almost giddy and he starts to speed up.

"Hey," I yell. "It may be easy for you to walk, but it isn't for me. Slow down, would ya?"

Cam looks back at me in that familiar, if friendly, sneer. "If we're late because you were walking too slow and I don't get a bed and I don't get any food, then we're going to have a real problem. Like the kind where I take those garbage clothes off you, try to sell them, and keep the money for my own personal food stash. And I'll be doing that while I rent out a crappy little motel room while you sleep on the porch."

"Pshhh," I mutter. "Like you could even get more than ten dollars for these pieces of crap."

"Yeah, yeah. Make fun of the man who is trying to get you into a bed tonight. That's cool. I get it," Cam says, and now his tone is a bit jarring.

"Whatever. I would have figured something out." This is the best I can offer.

"Just keep walking. We'll be there in a minute," Cam, ever determined, says.

I look up and in the direction of the shelter. It looks the same as ever. There's the nice glass financial towers not far to the left of it, and then the dilapidated brick and wood building of the shelter.

"Home sweet home!" Cam practically hums.

We approach the glass doors and pull them open. We walk into the main lobby and look around. Besides us, there aren't many people in here this evening. Maybe thirty to forty people.

"Where is everyone?" I ask Cam.

"What day is it today?" he asks me, right back, as he examines the room.

Beyond the front desk in the lobby is a digital clock.

6:25

Friday, September 2

"Ahh, that makes sense," Cam says as he keeps looking around.

"Why's that?" I ask, doing my own scanning around the lobby and mess hall.

"It's good for us. This means we will get a bed," he says.

"Why is hardly anyone here?" I ask again, now a bit exasperated because Cam has not answered my question.

"The first Friday of the month—in this case, September—is when everyone receives their welfare and social security checks. So that means the people who would normally stay in the shelter now have some money and the means to stay somewhere else tonight if they can." Cam sighs.

"So if that's the case . . . " I'm still staring at the clock as I ask my next question. " . . . why is it that you don't have a welfare check? Or I guess a better question . . . why are we not having a feast at McDonald's right now? I could be chowing down on a juicy McChicken and a Coke and some fries, and maybe a McFlurry." My mouth starts to salivate with each of those juicy, luscious words.

Cam just starts laughing, then coughing, then squeezing his

stomach. "Making me a little hungry there, too," he says with a facial expression that's equal parts ecstasy and pain at the same time. "Well, anyway, there is only about thirty-two minutes left for dinner, and I am dying of starvation. So why don't we hop in line?" Cam moves me toward the food line. "Also, we're very lucky. The night staff and security are different from the day shifts. So hopefully no one will recognize you from your outburst the other day, and we'll be able to eat dinner in peace."

"Agreed," I say, walking with Cam toward the front desk.

"Hi. I know we're late, but is there any way we could hop in line for dinner and secure bedding for tonight?" Cam asks.

The lady behind the desk looks swamped. The phone station she is at has five different blinking lights—I'm assuming these are all callers on hold—and she is also rifling through various piles of mail.

The woman says nothing and simply raises a finger to deliver a quiet expression. She continues sorting through the mail, and I keep looking back at the clock, which is changing second by second behind her.

"Miss, I really need to . . . "

The woman keeps scavenging through the mail while reaching for the phone bank and pressing one of the blinking light buttons.

"East Hills Shelter. Please hold for a moment." The woman snaps her eyes back toward me. Ever so briefly, I flinch.

"Name?"

"I . . . "

"Give me your name, sweetheart," she barks, aggravated.

"Oh . . . umm . . . Sam Case." My tone is soft.

"You're checked in for a bed tonight, sweetheart. Go hop in line really quick for some food."

"Oh, I also . . . "

The woman quickly moves the phone back to her face and continues sorting the mail. She reaches back to the phone bank and presses another button. "East Hill Shelter. Sorry for the hold. How may I direct your call today?"

I shrug and look at the small line of people waiting for food. There are only about twenty people in the mess hall. Many of them are already sitting, making small talk, eating their food. One man is sitting in the corner simply staring out the window as cars pass by. The rest of the people are playing cards, playing on cell phones, or sitting at the mess hall tables with their heads buried in their sleeves or coats.

I walk to the back of the line and look ahead at the dinner menu: "Fish Fillets with ambrosia and milk. Dessert served on the side."

"Ughh," I say at the thought of eating the shelter's ambrosia for a second time this month. All of a sudden, my stomach doesn't feel so great. I can just feel the ambrosia—a dessert of oranges and shredded coconut—going down my throat. I gag from reflex. I walk back to the front desk, and the woman is still taking calls and sorting through the mail piles.

"I'll wait until you're done," I say as I lean against the front desk.

She nods and shoos me toward the bench on the opposite side of the lobby entryway.

I watch as people hurry in and out of the busy glass doors. The red clock behind the counter ticks forward. I just sit there and watch. I look at the ground and close my eyes for a moment . . .

"Sweetheart?" A voice rings out from in front of me.

I shake my head out of my daze and look up. I glance up at the clock and then at the woman, who is motioning me to come forward. I slowly approach her.

The clock behind the woman now reads 7:02 P.M. "Did you need something, sweetheart? I am sorry for keeping you waiting, but I was really swamped with all this work. At 7 P.M. I always tell people I have more important things to attend to, then hang up the phones."

I look down at the woman's hands; all the piles of mail are neatly sorted. The desk is now clean from clutter.

"Sweetheart?" she says as she waves her hand in front of my face.

I shake my head to clear the daze once again. "Oh, sorry. I am a little out of it. Is there someone I can speak to about getting new bandages and gauze for my cheek and arm?"

The woman grimaces and then looks down toward the call station. "Oh. Sorry, sweetheart. The in-service nurse who works here on Fridays leaves at seven. I can call down to her office to see if I can catch her before she leaves, though."

I nod and smile but I'm holding back a bit of anger. *Maybe I could have seen the nurse if you weren't making so many damn calls,* I say in my head. I am, however, keeping up my smile.

"Alright, one moment," she says as she leans back in her chair and stares up at ceiling, and then back toward the large red clock. She picks up the phone and punches four numbers.

Twenty or so seconds elapses on the clock and there is no answer. "Ma'am . . . "

"Chelsea? Hi, Chelsea. I have a boy here who needs to have a quick checkup for an injury. Do you have time to look at him really quick?"

A moment passes. I hear some sort of words coming through the phone.

"I know you are just walking out the door. But this will be really quick, and this boy isn't in the best shape."

I let out a large exhale as I lean against the counter. *With my luck, she will probably leave and my jaw will fall off by tomorrow.*

"Oh, you'll see him!" The woman's face perks up and she motions for me to walk down the hall just past the front desk. "Alright, I will send him right now!" She hangs up the phone. "Alright, sweetheart. Just walk down the hall and take a left."

I walk toward the hallway entrance. The path is dimly lit. Both sides of the hall have large scuff marks going in various directions in a seemingly random pattern. This hall looks as if it has seen various fights, scuffles, and maybe worse.

I reach the end of the hall, turn left, and approach the only door with lights clearly still on inside. The sign next to the white doorframe reads: "Charge Station Nurse—volunteer." There is no name listed under the sign even though there's a small placard where a name could be inserted. I look inside and a woman in blue scrubs is standing but bending to read a computer screen.

"Umm, excuse me," I say as I take a slight step into the office.

"Sit on the table there and let me get a look at you," she says. She continues scrolling up and down on the computer screen in front of her.

I walk over to the small-sized patient table, push myself on top, and sit facing the general direction of the nurse. She pauses for a long second, then reaches above into a cabinet. The nurse is gorgeous. Long, flowing brown hair shimmering against the flickering light of the clinic above. So slim in figure. *I bet she has an amazing body underneath all those scrubs.* I let out a brief smile as I continue to watch her move back and forth, clambering upward against the cupboard, reaching for a packet of gauze.

She pulls out a clipboard and attaches two pieces of paper. She grabs a pencil and finally looks my way.

"Oh, wow," she says. She steps toward me with a grimace on her face and a look of concern.

I observe her beautiful face. Even more gorgeous than what I imagined while viewing her body. *Maybe I could get a date with her. God, I want to get a date with this woman. I am going to do it. I am going to ask her on a date. She won't know what hit her. This is your moment, Sam—seize it. And don't you dare wimp out.*

"Sweetheart. You smell awful." She lifts her nose into the air and inhales deeply. Her eyelashes flutter up and down. *God, she's so beautiful. Holy crap—I think I just realized what she said . . .* "It almost smells like rot or gangrene," she says.

I need to ask her on a date. Oh my god, I need to . . . shit—what did she say? Did she say 'gangrene'? Ahh, man, gangrene!—what about garbage? At least if I smell like garbage I can find a way to mask or get rid of the scent. I could hop in the shower really quick while she continues looking at the chart. Thirty seconds, tops . . . I could be back in this chair staring at this beautiful woman. Wait . . . what's my Aphrodite's name?

"Excuse me, miss. What's your name?" *I am an idiot. What did the lady at the front desk call her?*

"Call me Chelsea." Her cheeks widen and her glowing teeth finally break through her lips. Chelsea sighs as she exhales forcefully. She walks toward me. "Alright. Can I get your name really quick, first and last?"

"Samuel Case," I exclaim, a bit of pride in my voice. Forcefully, I push all the air into my chest and push it outward.

"Alright." She makes a quick note on her clipboard. "So, have you received medical attention, Samuel?"

"Call me Sam," I say, a small smile on my face.

The nurse looks up at me briefly and smiles again. *Jackpot. Don't freak out, Sam. You got this. Just keep the conversation flowing.*

"Alright, Sam. The bandages on your face look as though they have been administered by a medical professional. Have you been in the hospital lately, or have you been to urgent care?" The woman looks up again for a moment as her eyes trace down the side of my right cheek. Those eyes are a gorgeous teal-green. I could almost sleep in them . . .

"Sam?" she asks as she cocks her head slightly.

"Ahh, umm, yeah. I was there two days ago for a cut to my cheek."

"OK. And what about your arm?"

My arm is now actually a purplish-brown color.

"That's something that happened a long time ago," I express as I rub the joint area of the arm back and forth.

"It looks pretty fresh to me," she says as she continues taking notes. "Alright, let's see this cut." She places her clipboard on the linoleum countertop and reaches out with her hands out. She gently lifts her hands against my face and turns my face slightly sideways. Her hands feel . . . soft, comfortable, peaceful . . . I close my eyes and put my weight into my face as I lean against her hands. *She reminds me of . . .*

"Sam, I am going to remove the bandage to see how the cut looks. Is that OK?"

"Anything for you," I say, pretty much in a dreamlike stupor.

"Um, OK," she says, chuckling lightly. "Well, here we go." Slowly, extremely slowly, she pulls the bandage away from the blackened skin underneath. The adhering glue tethering the bandage to my face grips with all its strength.

I grit my teeth—hard—as she slowly coaxes the bandage away. Bit by bit, the exposed flesh screams upon contact with the air. My soul wants to scream in agony. *That's not an option. Be strong; she can't see how weak you are. How vulnerable you are . . . I need to be strong. I need to show some bravado.* I peer out the corner of my right eye. The nurse's happy complexion turns. Now she is grimacing. Her teeth press into each other as she bites the inner part of her lip.

"Do you know how many stitches the doctors gave you?" she asks, slowly rotating my face back and forth.

"No. I was out while they were doing them."

"OK. Well, it looks like this is getting infected. I am going to give you some antibiotics that we have on hand, but this won't be enough to help you fully. The supply is only enough through Monday. On Monday, you need to go up to urgent care on the hill and see if they can give you some antibiotics. I will make a call on your behalf. As for your arm, I will give you some ibuprofen to avoid the pain, but I don't want you sharing with anyone. Do you understand?"

I nod in agreement as she returns to her clipboard and makes a variety of notes.

"Also, I want to redress your cut, but you are extremely dirty, as you can see."

As her eyes move up and down, I follow them. She's right. I am covered in a variety of stains, dirt, and probably alcohol from spitting up the whiskey. Grass stains cover my sweats and my white T-shirt. In fact, the T-shirt is no longer white—it's more like a beige hue plastering the white. I am a wreck.

The nurse gazes down at her wrist, examining her watch. She looks at her computer and then back at her watch. "How quickly do you think you can take a shower?"

"I don't know. I can probably take one in about five minutes," I say, sounding unsure, probably even to myself.

"It will have to do," she squawks as she motions me up from the table and toward the door. "I will try and get you a change of clothes. Just please hurry in the shower so I can head home at a reasonable time. I want to redress your cut before I leave." I nod. She pushes me out the door and immediately slams it shut behind me.

Alright. Now to make myself look pretty. I walk down the hallway toward the communal shower area.

The shelter is set up in a somewhat odd fashion. On the main floor—the ground floor—is the mess hall, the lobby, and the hallways leading to the offices: administration, nursing, and a few other offices. The sleeping quarters and showers are on the second floor alongside a large room with lockers for staff, volunteers, and residents.

I walk back to the main area where the mess hall and front lobby are stationed. I glance at the clock.

7:30

The mess area is closed. People are still dawdling about—sitting around in the main lobby, making idle chitchat, playing games, or doing some other random form of entertainment.

"Everything good, sweetheart?" rings out a voice to my right.

I peer over my shoulder. There sits the woman at the front desk, the one who helped me earlier. She is looking at me hopefully.

"Everything is all good," I say, cheerily, as I turn my body toward the stairs next to the hallway. I slowly climb the stairs as I hold onto the railing with my left hand. The cut on my cheek still burns from being exposed to the air, and no amount of clamping my jaw shut is helping quell the pain. As I reach the landing, I can hear the woman at the front desk mumbling to someone else.

"He's in . . . shape . . . new clothes." These are the only words I can make out as I trudge up the second half-flight of stairs.

This shower is going to feel like Heaven from above.

The top of the stairs opens into a large bathroom full of lockers and showers. I walk toward one of the benches, sit down, and let out a large exhale. My ears prick. It sounds as if there is only one other person in the locker room. But it doesn't matter; they are on the far side, a good distance from where I am. The room is quiet and peaceful; the only sound comes from the humming of the lights above and the occasional drip of water from the many leaky shower faucets. I close my eyes and lean forward. I rest my head against the cool metal from the lockers and let out a large breath.

For the next five minutes, I do nothing—absolutely nothing. My thoughts filter in and out. I suck in a large breath, hold it, then exhale slowly. Finally, I press myself to my feet. I slog my way toward the communal showers. I turn the closest shower knob to hot. The water pushes out slowly at first, then begins ricocheting off the tile floor as it increases with speed. I trudge back to the lockers, open one, remove my clothing, slowly, and carefully place it in the locker. I shut the locker door, placing both hands against the lock and pushing my body weight into it. I hear a satisfying click.

I grab a towel from one of the racks adjacent to the shower entrance and throw it on one of the towel holders inside the shower. Without so much as a thought, I jump into the steamy water. I close my eyes.

Slowly, I rest my head against the cool metal tower the water is flowing from. The water slides down my back and alongside my ears as I breathe in and out. Each movement of breath soothes the rest of my aching body. I erect my spine. Exhaling deeply, I rip the bandage clinging to my face—exposing it to the air once more. *Interesting. It doesn't sting nearly as bad this time.* I run my fingers alongside the cut. The edges of the cut, bumpy and raised, cusp at the top and push slightly outward. I exhale forcefully two more times and close my eyes. All I see is black as I lower my head into the streaming water.

I am pretty sure the nurse said, "Please don't expose the cut to water" on the way out. But I don't care. I am in pain.

The water seeps into the cut and I burst out in an explosion of pain. I sink to my knees and flex my hands into fist formations. *"Ahhh, fuck!"* I scream. I open my eyes to look toward the ground. A diluted stream of blood slowly makes its way toward the drain along with some other precarious-looking fluid, which is yellow. I exhale slowly and the pain starts to fade a bit. I can feel some of the excess water seeping in through the cut and into my mouth. I slowly massage the cut back and forth along the grooves to make it calm. I close my eyes again and rub the cut back and forth; I try to time the rubbing with the exhalation of my breaths.

And then I hear him . . . or, *it.*

"Well, well, well. Ain't this a sight for sore eyes? It's my gorgeous little camper. And how are we doing today?"

A shiver shoots down my back as the words sting my ears. My eyes fly open and I immediately whip my body around toward the shower opening. In a moment, my legs go weak, my heart shudders and drops, and my eyes constrict in fear.

"Well, well now, Sammy. Don't say you didn't miss me?"

I take a deep swallow as the man steps into the shower and flashes a sick smile. His grotesque teeth plaque and yellow teeth reflect the incandescent light above.

"Why are you here? Get away from me," I say as I slowly position myself to put the shower tower between him and me.

"Now, now, now . . . that's not very polite, is it?"

It's him—the asshole who followed me up on that roof. The man who cut my cheek. The man who stabbed Cam. The man who made me go through all this pain. The man who raped me when I thought everything was going to be OK. The man who left me alone up there . . .

"Leave me alone!" I scream as I further position the water tower between myself and him. He slowly enters the shower area. The dirt from the bottom of his torn boots soils the water below. He looks down and kicks some of the water in a playful manner.

"Sammy. Why the hostility? I have missed you so much. Our last interaction . . . well, let's just say it left me wanting more." The man licks his lips several times; it is sickening. "See, at first, I couldn't put my finger on it. What on earth made little Sammy . . . just so . . . " The man looks toward the ceiling in thought as he caresses the bottom of his cheek. "Just so . . . delicious." The man's laugh seems to cover any water noise coming from the shower. He takes a step forward. I simultaneously take a step back as my hands hit the cold tile wall behind. *No, no, no. I'm trapped.* "It's funny. I can't stop thinking about our beautiful night together—looking at the beautiful skyline of our gorgeous city. And then it came to me. I know why I can't get you off my mind. It's the crazy in your eyes. Let's just say that it drives *me* . . . crazy. Don't you think you should come greet me?" he says in a twisted voice.

He takes a few forceful steps in my direction. With each step he gets closer. I push my hands into the wall, edging myself off to one side. As he clears the left side of the tower, I spring forward. *There's no way he can cover this much ground that quickly.* And then I feel a strong constriction wrap itself around my arm. I look down in terror as I see the man's hand cusped around my forearm.

"I really think that it is in your best interest if you just play along," he says, his tone deep and forceful.

"*Get off!*" I yell.

"Hey! Knock it off!" booms a voice in the distance.

The man and I look toward the source of those words: a large black man dressed in a security uniform. A shiny silver name tag—"Boris"— stands out. He is at the top of the stairs with a pile of clothing reaching to his face. He's wearing a pair of black Crocs.

"Don't make me repeat myself," the big man says as he quickly places the clothing on a table to his side and carefully approaches the shower opening.

The monster averts his gaze from Boris to me. "Well now, Sammy. I guess it isn't the time and place for our next play date. Another time, then. Hopefully you treat me with a little more respect at our next reunion." The man licks his lips and lets out a large, gaseous exhale.

I can feel my body convulse from the smell of his breath. "Next time, dreamer," the man says as he quickly steps away from me and toward the security guard.

"Sorry there, boss." He looks the guard up and down. "Boris! That's it: Boris. I just wanted to have a chat with my little friend. I'll be on my way now."

The man steps to the side of Boris and shimmies his way around him.

Boris crosses his arms and stands firm until the man has completely navigated around him. He then turns his gaze toward me. "Are you Sam Case?"

I just stand there. My heart is racing. I can feel the blood draining out of my face. Each second the blood pumps out of my legs—there is less and less strength. Not only am I alone, I am naked, afraid, open, and exposed. If it hadn't been for Boris, I don't know what would have happened.

"Hey, boy!" Boris raises his voice. "Are you Sam Case?"

I slowly nod, pulling myself a bit out of my state of shock. "Um, yes."

The man points toward the pile of clothes. "These clothes are from the nurse downstairs. She wants you down there immediately so she can get you fixed up. You better hurry so I don't have to come back up here."

"Uh, yeah sure," I say as I place my hand against the tower to keep my footing. My vision blurs as the white tiles slowly fade to black. Stars circle about in my field of vision.

Boris turns his back to me and starts walking toward the stairs. A deep, stressed inhale works its way into my throat as I try to control my breathing. Pulse by pulse, the breaths are coming out in a frantic manner. *I need to stop hyperventilating. My hands, my legs, everything feels weak. Damnit!* The shudder and tingle down my spine won't stop. I wander back under the water shooting from the water tower. I do nothing. *I am nothing.* I stand there as the water continues to run down my back and seep its way into my mouth. *Nothing.* No burning sensation, no dreadful pain—just pure adrenaline. I bury my hands in my face. Tears cascade, joining the downpouring water.

Red fluid begins dripping down the side of my hands and falling off when enough accumulates—*so much blood.* I lift my right hand to my face and caress the bumpy ridges of the cut. I lower my hand and look at the tips of my fingers. Blood covers the cusp of my fingers and leaks onto the back side, along my fingernails. *My heart rate must have gotten my blood flowing. That must be why I am bleeding so much from the cut. With this hot water, I am probably not in the best situation.* I take a deep breath in, partially drawing some of the shower water into my mouth. I swash it around inside my mouth. I'm immediately met with the taste of blood and water. I can feel the warm draw of the mixed fluids leaking out of the cut and down and off my face to the drain below.

I slowly turn the faucet off. I press my hand against my face. I turn toward the placement of my towel at the entrance, hoping to wipe away some of the blood. I lunge for my . . .

"Phewwww!!" All I see is the tile ceiling above. I watch in slow motion as my feet rise above my eye line. With what seems like extreme precision, I feel each individual body part slam against the ground. First, my head—with a large thud. Followed by my back and both arms. Finally, my legs.

I roll my eyes back and forth as I slowly watch stars form in my view. My head rolls up and down—tracing the ceiling tiles. The room is blurry. I can feel something warm filling in my mouth once again, and now running down my neck. It feels good, almost filling.

My eyes shoot open and I immediately sit up. My stomach gouges upward. I spit at the floor. A large upchuck of blood flies out of my mouth.

"Case—I swear to *god!*" The voice rings out in the distance.

I quickly turn my head, in a daze, toward the voice. "Didn't I tell you? . . . " Boris's voice echoes off the tiles and punctures my ears.

Through the daze and stars, I see Boris's face. A look of shock and concern. "Jesus, son. What the hell happened to you?"

Boris grabs the towel hanging on the wall and slowly walks over to me while trying to avoid the puddles of bloody water across the floor.

He kneels and slowly hands me the towel.

"Son, what happened?" Boris tilts his head to the side and grimaces at the sight of the cut. "We better get you down to the nurse quick. She will fix you right up—hopefully."

I continue to stare in a daze as Boris extends his hand. He slowly lifts me to my feet. "Are you OK to walk?"

I don't have enough energy to lift my head. All I can see is the slow drip of blood running off my chin and hitting the floor. "Yeah, I'm fine. Thanks, man. I appreciate it." It's a mess of gargled words, but at least I got them out.

Boris releases his hand from my forearm and makes his way out of the shower. I drape the towel around my body, only slightly covering myself. I look toward the towel, patches of blood now mixed with the white.

"Alright. Let's sit you down right here. I will go grab the nurse from downstairs to see what she says." Boris quickly jumps to his feet, once again stares at me with a look of concern, and then rapidly heads down the stairs.

I stare forward at the blue lockers. The only thing I can see with certainty are the metal hinges erupting from the right side of the lockers. Each gleams in the light—and this hurts my eyes. The metal benches are cool to the touch of my bare legs. The air in the locker room is frigid and my skin turns to goosebumps. I gaze down at my bare legs. Little deltas of blood and water are forming on their way to the floor. I look across the locker room to a small mirror that stands erect from the floor. A young, tattered man stares back at me—his face has too much flowing blood. His body looks scarred and weathered. His hair is full but thin. His eyes look timorous and aged. *What has happened to me?* My eyes begin to water at the sight of myself. *I can't do this anymore.* I look toward the mirror again. "I can't do this!" I scream as I collapse my face in my hands.

"Yeah, he's up here!" It's Boris's voice from a distance. "He is pretty banged up. You're gonna want to take a look at him."

The sounds of heavy and light footsteps echo off the walls as they hurry into the locker room. I release my face from the cradle of my hands. I slightly turn my head, in a stupor, and lock eyes with Chelsea. I try to let out a brief smile. I can feel the blood covering my front teeth while I try to mask the anguish inside. Her face does not match my greeting. No . . . she has a look of concern and a slight look of disappointment.

"Jesus. Sam, what the hell happened?" she asks as she approaches and drops to one knee.

I smile at her again—tears running down my face and blood leeching out of my cheek.

"Sweetheart, as much as I love your smile, I need to know what happened to you. Do I need to call an ambulance?"

I instinctively reach for her arm as she lifts it to touch my face. At that moment, I see Boris twitch and reach for his walkie-talkie. Chelsea calmly relaxes her hand and lowers it to her side. I look Chelsea directly in the eyes. Her face is stoic, nearly expressionless. I look deep into those teal-green eyes.

"No hospital," I say in a garbled mess of tears, snot, and agony.

"We'll see about that," she says, perhaps reluctantly. She steadily raises my flexed arm with her other arm, releases my grip, and slowly lowers my arm to the side. "I am going to look at your cut. Are you fine with that?"

I nod my head slowly as the taste of salt and water drips into my mouth.

She tilts my head to the side, slowly examining up and down. "Your cut is still bleeding profusely, but it seems as though all the stitches are still intact."

"What does that mean?" I ask.

"It means you don't have to go to the hospital. Well, that is, unless there is something else horribly wrong with you."

As her words tumble out, I can feel my body slowly start to relax. Chelsea reaches into the first aid bag hanging from her shoulder against her torso. Quickly sorting through the satchel, she pulls out some weird towelettes. She quickly rips through the plastic wax lining and softly places them against the grooves of the cut. A sting shoots down the side of my face at contact. "Hold here," she says as she continues digging through the first aid bag.

Through the fibers of the towelettes, I can feel blood rushing inward. With each moment, the fibrous patch becomes heavier.

"Hold that right there while I keep searching, Sam." She continues rummaging through the bag. Now her face is twitching in anger. "Finally! Here. This will be easier if I can place this on the bench and open it up."

Boris is standing next to Chelsea and watching as she continues to treat me. "Umm, excuse me, Boris. Can you please move so I can open this up?"

"Oh, yes ma'am," he says, surprised, and takes a large step to the right.

With the towelettes full, more blood rushes inward—now back into my mouth. I can feel the blood swelling in my mouth. The taste of phlegm has become sickening. I open my mouth wide and spew blood on the floor. Boris jumps back—as Chelsea is *still* searching through that bag.

"Jesus, kid! Let me know when you are about to do that!" Boris's high-pitched voice makes Chelsea chuckle a little.

"How much blood is draining into your mouth?" Chelsea asks while quickly whipping out a small flashlight from her pocket. "Alright. Open up."

I shrug as I slowly open my mouth. It seems as though tendrils of blood, mucus, and saliva are all pulling until taught. "I don't know," I manage to mumble. "Enough for me to get sick of the taste and spit it up."

"Yeah, but that doesn't take that much, does it? Now keep your mouth open!" Chelsea holds the bottom part of my chin with one hand as she reaches blindly into the first aid kit. Without looking, she pulls out a plastic packet of Neosporin. She clutches the bag in her teeth and shears the top open to the side. With her free hand, she grasps it and squeezes. A small portion of gelatinous liquid oozes to the top. "Open up wider."

"I can't. It hurts too much." A hot pulse of pain shoots down my mouth and into my neck.

"Fine. Then stick out your tongue. This is going to hurt when I lace this on the inside. If anything, please, don't lick it until it's all gone. Then I won't get to go home and you are going to be in a mountain of pain. Understand?"

I nod as she clutches the bottom of my chin tighter. My tongue flops out lethargically.

"Boris, would you do me a quick favor? Can you put some of the Neosporin on the tip of my index finger really quick?"

Boris's face, squeamish from the blood and phlegm, now looks ghostly white. "Oh, yes ma'am. Right away, ma'am." Boris takes a small step closer. Clumsily, he grabs the Neosporin. "Umm, where do you want this, ma'am?" he says, asking what she's already told him. Boris's deep, low voice is simply a cover. He's a big baby and scared of a little blood.

"Just right on my finger. Quickly, please," Chelsea barks.

Boris's shoulders jolt upward. "Oh, yes ma'am!" He lowers the Neosporin just above her finger and squeezes out a tiny amount.

Chelsea looks at her finger with disappointment. "More, please."

Boris's hands are now noticeably shakier. He squeezes out an ample amount.

"Thanks, Boris," she says as she turns her attention back to me. "Alright. I am going to coat the inside of the cut with this. Do not lick it away or you will start bleeding again. Do you understand?"

I nod my head. Cringing at the newest onrush of pain, I push my mouth as open as I can.

Chelsea pulls my tongue out farther, making the inside of my mouth scream in pain. *"Oww!"* Second after second, she coats the gooey substance against the inside of the cut. For a moment it hurts, badly, then the coolness of the fluid kicks in. The pain slowly starts to subside. She removes her hand from inside my mouth and continues to peer at the cut from the outside. Satisfied with her work, she rubs her hands together quickly. "Alright. Better?"

Working hard to keep my tongue away from the goo, I slowly nod.

"OK. Now this part is going to sting. Just do everything in your power not to open your mouth, and please don't lick the Neosporin off from the inside. I don't think either of us wants me sticking my hand in your mouth again."

I exhale forcefully.

"I am going to take that as a 'Yes, Chelsea, I'll do anything you say!'" she says, chuckling.

She slowly removes a white-labeled bottle from the first aid kit. The bottle reads: Hydrogen Peroxide, 3%. "OK, this is really going to sting, but I need you to stay still." She looks deep in my eyes. "I need you to nod to confirm."

I nod. She quickly opens the bottle and douses a large amount of fluid into one of the available towels. "Ready?"

Again, I nod. I don't have any other choice.

She places the towel against my cut.

Fire. My cheek is literally on fire. Every single nerve in my cheek screams in pain as the individual fibers from the towel sear them. Inside my head I can hear the scream of a man in pain—from mountains away. I swallow: a huge, hard gulp. The pit of my throat tears at my blood-soaked esophagus.

"Just a little bit more." Chelsea rubs the towel along the edges of the cut. Tears stream down my face alongside the cut.

My eyes shuttle back and forth; maybe this will alleviate some of the pain. *Just end already. Just end!* I squeeze my legs as hard as I can. My hands flex so hard the whites of my knuckles show.

"Sweetheart, relax your face," Chelsea says as she continues rubbing the cut.

How the fuck am I supposed to relax my face with you rubbing fire into it? You don't tell someone to stop being cold while they're freezing to death!

I close my eyes and vault them even further shut in my mind's eye. I spit up some blood from my mouth and then . . . it's over. The pain slowly starts to recede as the outside of my face slowly pulses back to normal.

"OK then!" Chelsea lets out a large sigh and an exhale. "Now that it is all clean, I'm going to bandage it for you, then have you meet me down in the office. Sound good?" Chelsea stares into my eyes. "I am serious, Sam. If I have to clean this cut for a third time . . . " She flexes her hands and her neck constricts. " . . . I will whoop your ass."

I do nothing for the next five minutes. I stare at the metal lockers and can feel the insertion of various bandages on my face. Each layer feels more secure. It all slowly begins to hurt less and less.

"Alright, all done. Is there anything else that is hurting or open that I should look at before I see you downstairs?"

I swallow to open my mouth.

"That was a rhetorical question. I will finish up with you when you come downstairs. Just, please, hurry up. Do you think you'll need help getting downstairs?"

I turn my head toward her and am met by those teal-green eyes. I shake my head slowly back and forth; once again, I can feel tears starting to come. "I think I'll be OK."

Chelsea's demeanor changes as she packs up the first aid bag. "I am so sorry, Sam. Nothing like this should happen to someone your age."

She stops packing and looks back at me. She smudges her face and lips. "You'll be OK, sweetheart. We will get you on some antibiotics and some ibuprofen and you will feel right as rain."

Chelsea seals the first aid kit and heads for the stairs. Boris, still standing next to her, moves to the side to make room for her. "I'll walk down with you," he mumbles. The color has started to return to his face.

Chelsea gives a small smile as they work their way to the stairs.

"Poor kid. I feel bad for him." I hear Boris mumble the words.

I trudge over to the pile of clothes. The blood flowing from inside my cheek has finally halted. I push black sweatpants over my legs and slowly pull a clean white shirt over my face, taking care not to graze the suturing around the cut. I reach for the socks on the bench.

"Sam?" A voice rings out from the top of the stairs. "What happened to you? Are you alright?" I slowly adjust my body to the turn toward the questioner.

Cam stands at the top of the stairs; he is staring at the trail of blood leading from the showers to the bench, just left of where I am sitting. "What . . . what happened?"

I lower myself onto the bench and lift my legs slowly to fit the socks on my feet. "What happened?" Cam keeps asking this question as I pull the socks on.

"He was here." The words come slurring out of my mouth.

"*Who?*" Cam demands.

"The man . . . the man . . . the man . . . "

"*What* man? Which man? Who are you talking about?" A look of panic begins to overtake Cam.

"The man that raped me!" I yell, finally.

Cam stares at the ground. His face seems in shock. He slowly walks to where I'm sitting. He places his hand against my shoulder as he lowers himself onto the bench.

"That man . . . " I mutter, once more, in a hushed tone.

"What about him?" Cam says as he leans closer to me.

"He deserves to die." The tantalizing sounds fall from my mouth and echo against the floor. *Death . . . this man deserves death. This man needs to die. Die, die, die!* A melodic chant resonates inside my head. Each time, more hypnotic and intoxicating. "He needs to die. He is going to die." I push myself up from the bench and begin walking toward the stairs.

"What? Wait, Sam. What did you say?" Cam's voice echoes around the shower as the backdrop of water hitting the tile also is heard.

"Sam! Wait! Don't be hasty! You haven't thought of the repercussions! Sam!"

No. I know what I have to do.

SEVENTEEN

THE DAY

"Sam, you can't do that. It won't solve anything." Cam's words echo around inside my head. "Getting even with him or even killing him won't solve anything. We need to go to the cops!"

I grit my teeth and rub my tongue against the cut on my cheek—there is still no respite from the persistent ache. Scar tissue has formed in a cusp around the outside of the cut. *I'm gonna kill him . . . I'm gonna kill him . . . I'm gonna kill him.* This chant, incessant, goes off in my head. I don't want to stop—with each utterance I feel more powerful, more assured, more confident.

* * * * *

It's a day later. I bury my head in my coat and lower my chin. I pace toward the door to the East Hills Shelter. I walk through the two automatic doors and into the well-lit mess hall. I glance around. *Where is he?* People have started lining up for lunch. I gaze over at the main desk and see Susan sifting through some notes. "Hi, sweetheart! How are you today?" she asks.

I shrug my shoulders, burying myself further in my coat, and continue walking forward. She reaches out quickly and grabs my shoulder. "Sweetheart! How are you doing today?" I glance at her and can see her eyes expanding from staring at my cut. "Sam, what the hell happened? Are you OK?" Without warning, she grabs my face and slightly twists it to the left. Her pupils seem to narrow as she squints her eyes. She slowly traces her finger around the cut and then peers up at my forehead to see a similar cut. "Sam, what happened? Do you need me to get anything for you?" I slowly shrug and turn my body away from her. "Sam!" At her outburst, many of the people lounging in the mess hall turn their attention in my direction. Everyone is staring. I turn back to Susan.

"I'm fine. Don't worry about it." I quickly turn my back to her. I walk to the back of the line that's formed and waiting for food. The two security guards across the room eye me as I stand there—I am trying to keep my gaze forward. *Shit. Just leave me alone. Don't screw with me today.* The two men whisper something to one another and then start walking toward me. *Damnit.*

They approach. One is a large black man with tattoos ranging down his arms, and the other is a smaller white male with a tattoo ring covering the circumference of his neck. The men come within a couple feet of me and blow out their chests and tighten their backs. They stare down at me, and finally the white man with the neck tattoo speaks up. "Alright, little man, we don't want any trouble out of you today. If you pull any stunts like you did the other day, you're done. That will be your final strike. Do you understand?"

I remain silent and just stare ahead, right down the line. "Hey! He's talking to you!" demands the other security guard. "You going to answer me? Or are we going to have a problem?" The man lowers himself to my cheek height, places his hand on my shoulder, and smiles. "You better answer me, boy." He tightens his grip on my shoulder.

"Ahh, gentlemen, gentlemen. He'll definitely behave, officers." A voice has risen from behind my shoulder. Another hand pushes down on my shoulder from behind. I rapidly turn my head back to see Mr. P's illuminating teeth caps shining—they reflect the incandescent light of the bulbs above. "Ain't that right, big man?" Mr. P stares down at me, quite intently, from behind a pair of sunglasses.

I look back at the security guards and then back at Mr. P. They all look on—all eagerly awaiting an answer. "Yes sir," I whisper quietly.

"A little louder, boy!" demands the white security guard as he tightens his grip on my shoulder. The pressure of his grip digs into the deep muscle of my shoulder girdle. "Ahh! Oww!" I cringe as I start contorting my body to avoid the pressure.

"Yes, sir!" I belt out. The officer slowly relaxes his grip and then turns back to the first officer.

"Behave yourself, son," the officers say, nearly in unison, as they both turn and walk away. "If he does anything, Mr. P, it's on you too," the officers mutter as they head back to the security office across the room.

Mr. P, whose hand is still planted against my shoulder, twists my body, turning my chest toward him. I look up into those sunglass-covered eyes. "Sammy, it's probably in your best interest—and now mine—to stay calm today. You heard the man. One more strike and you're out, and there goes one of your only sources of food. And if you get me kicked out, stopping me from getting my food, the 'P' in my name is going to change to something else. Also, the people are a little on edge with your presence today, so I would keep it on the down low." I turn my head to survey the room and examine everyone. Everyone does seem twitchy, on edge. It seems like the slightest disruption could kick off a riot.

I turn my head back to see Mr. P looking at me intently, smiling. "Let's just enjoy this meal, Sammy! Sound good?"

I nod my head, casually, in agreement. He releases his grip on my shoulder and we both stand there in line. I look at the metal lifts between the kitchen and the mess hall. A door bursts open on the left-hand side of the metal lifts and a cart loaded with pastries, chocolates, and cake is pushed into the mess hall. The loud screech of the rusty wheels draws everyone's attention. The person pushing the cart is . . . the boy I had jerked upward at the cart the other day. *Wow, I am surprised he came back. Most people would have cut and run if attacked by one of us.* Mr. P leans over my shoulder. "Be especially nice to that one." Mr. P smiles; I can smell his minty breath spiral around my face and into my nose.

"Alright, alright," I reply, though my tone is rushed, short.

The metal lifts rise up to the ceiling and the giant windows to the kitchen screech open. Dozens of servers line up on the opposite side of the gate and a loud bell rings behind them. "Lunch is now served! Line up!" Any remaining people lounging in the mess hall stand and start walking to the line that had already begun to expand outside the shelter and into the streets. Various people try to cut in line, but the more aggressive patrons immediately push them out. The security officers walk back and forth, dealing with anyone making an unwelcomed move.

I glance back at the boy behind the cart. My eyes meet his. He swallows harshly. I sigh and then look at the ground; I feel ashamed. I raise my head, away from the view of the dessert boy, and survey the room. *Nothing. He's not here.* I grit my teeth. *He better be here.* I look down at my knuckles. The whites clearly press outward as I clench my fists.

The line slowly moves forward. A small scuffle breaks out every now and then, but for the most part, everything moves ahead slowly. The meal is beef enchiladas and some sort of soup, with bread and dessert. The smell of processed fruit wafts through the air. I grab a tray and set it on the metal railing. As I move down the line, I notice each of the servers eyeing me carefully. One a look of disgust, another a look of fear, and several other expressions of disapproval. Of eight of them, occasionally one would sneer at me and then turn away immediately after serving me. I get about three-fourths of the way down the line when one of the servers looks me dead in the eyes.

"Next!" he yells, then looks right past me. I stand there about to open my mouth when Mr. P grabs my shoulder. "Keep on moving, big man." I close my mouth and grind my teeth. *Jackass doesn't have the right to deny me food.* I reach the dessert cart and glance back at the line of servers. Every one of them stops serving and glares at me. I turn back toward the boy serving desserts. While my head was turned, he had backed up half a step.

"Just take whatever you want," he says with a quiet voice.

I look up at him. "I'm sorry. I didn't mean to lash out at you."

The boy stands there—paralyzed. I wait for a moment and he

doesn't say anything. I try once more. "Like I said, sorry."

"Just keep moving, Sam. Maybe another day." Mr. P nudges me away from the dessert cart and out onto the general mess hall floor. I look around for a table. My usual spot—the far side of the mess hall with a small window overlooking Main Street—is empty. I take a small step forward. A voice rings out to my right.

"Hey there, cupcake. Why don't you come and sit next to me?" Chills shoot down my spine and my knuckles clench the plastic tray tighter. The cut in my cheek burns as the muscles in my face constrict. I can feel my heartbeat pump and pulse. I clench my face. My eyes water. His breath floods the air around me. With each shallow breath in, my body rejects the foreign smell. The man bursts into laughter and slams a palm against the open seat next to him. "Why don't you take a seat!" He leans closer to me and just stares.

I'm in shock. My tray is trembling and I can feel my chest expand and shrink with each breath. "It's in your best interest," the man says as he briefly moves a couple of inches to his left to make more room at the end of the bench.

A hand places itself on my shoulder and nudges me forward. "Just keep moving, Sam." It's Mr. P within inches of my backside. "Best leave the trash to where it sits." Mr. P flexes his brow and stares at the man.

I turn back to see the man once again locking eyes with me. "Enjoy the rest of your day," he says with a chuckle. The man's breath becomes shallower and he seems to take a large, hissing inhale. "Tonight isn't going to be a fun night for you," he says, smiling ear to ear, which just exposes his rotten front teeth. My breath trembles and my tray shakes more and more as the adrenaline pumps ferociously through my body.

"Just keep moving, big man," Mr. P says again, nudging me forward with his elbow and knee.

We sit at "my" table in the back. Mr. P places his tray on the opposite side of the table and looks me in the eyes. "It was him, wasn't it?" Mr. P turns his head back over his shoulder to look at the man. The man is sitting with a small group of people—cracking jokes and laughing manically. He turns his head to look at me. I just stare down at my tray. Mr. P turns his gaze back to me with a look of dismay. "You alright, Sammy. You're white as a ghost, and it looks like you might go to the bathroom right here and now."

My heart rate slows as the adrenaline quietly settles out of my hands and body. Feeling and sensation leech back into my hands. Tears begin to form. I grind my teeth.

"You should eat something, Sammy. Get your strength back." Mr. P takes off his sunglasses, places them on the table, and pushes my tray at me. "Eat!" He stares at his food, quickly lifts a piece of bread to his mouth, and rips part of it away.

"Give me your knife," I say to him, my voice monotone.

Mr. P, in the middle of swallowing, immediately coughs. He hits his chest multiple times, coughing out a mixture of phlegm, saliva, and half-chewed bread morsels. "What?" I stare straight in his eyes. Mr. P's eyes are bloodshot from lack of oxygen. "Sammy, you don't want to do anything like that! That will be the end of the road for you, and there is no way to know that someone won't try to stab you once you do it."

I scrape my front teeth on the back side of my bottom teeth. "I don't care. He has taken everything from me," I say, tears now rushing down my face and dropping to the table below.

"Sammy, I don't . . . " I quickly lift my hands to my face and peel off the bandaging and gauze covering the cut. On viewing the cut, Mr. P cringes and almost gags up the small amount of bread he's consumed.

"I wasn't able to do anything that night, but I can definitely do something now," I begin to say to him. "Who am I to say that I was the first he has harmed? Let's say he gets bored with me—finally leaves me alone. Who's to say that he won't hunt down another . . . and then another . . . and then another? He won't be able to hurt anybody again." I stare at Mr. P again, even more determination in my face. Every muscle flexes, every muscle tugs more tightly at the cut in my cheek.

"Give me your knife now!" I slam my hand against the table.

"Sam . . . I won't."

"Give it to me!" I demand as I avert my gaze to the monster on the other side of the room.

Mr. P sighs, his face weighing every word. He swallows multiple "I'm sorry, big man." Mr. P drops the knife into my hand as he slowly looks back down at his food. He continues feeding small bits of bread into his mouth, but there is no swallowing, no chewing, no movement.

He looks up at me once more. "Good-bye, Sammy."

I rise to my feet and clutch the knife on the inside of my coat. I step over the bench and peer down at Mr. P. His face is blank—no emotion, just staring into oblivion.

I walk to where the man is sitting. He now looks up at me in a smile. "Oh, I see you've made the right decision," he chuckles as he lightly pats the empty seat next to him. He gazes up at my face. The smile on his face creeps inward and the muscles on his face flex. "That's a dangerous look you got there, son. You might want to change it before you get hurt." The man reaches up and yanks my left arm down—rapidly pulling me toward the bench.

For a moment, everything seems to move in slow motion. I peer back toward Mr. P. "I'm sorry," I mouth in his direction.

"What's that, boy?" demands the man as he leans over me. He places his right arm around my right shoulder and exhales forcefully—fully aware I can't stand the smell of his breath.

My eyes narrow as I try to close off my nose and mouth to prevent the invasion of this awful stench. "One more time," demands the man as he leans in closer.

An utterance of nonsense peels out from under my breath. The man leans in closer. I take a large, deep breath. My heart pounds as adrenaline surges through my body. What feels like forever only lasts a split-second or two. I reach into my pocket as he curls his face closer to my mouth. I grasp my hand around the serrated edge of the knife and slowly edge my way down toward the grip. Once I reach it, I position my hand tightly around the grip and squeeze. My heart slows as the noise from the room drowns itself out in the thud of my heartbeat.

"I honestly didn't catch that last part, boy. It seems like you have something important to tell me." The man's ear is now inches from my mouth.

"I do. *Die.*"

I jolt my left hand up and squeeze his neck with all the force in my arm. His head cocks backward as I quickly rise to my feet. His eyes immediately become bloodshot. "What are you doing, you little shit!" I turn my head with suddenness both right and left. Immediately, the people sitting next to us rip the knives out of their pockets and hold them in a braced position. The usual sounds of the cafeteria lunch-room go silent.

"Hey! What are you doing over there," screams a voice from behind my shoulder. "Let go of him!" Heavy footsteps pound in my direction.

I quickly look back at the man. His eyes lock on mine, a small smile blanketing his face. He clutches his arms around my hands that are squeezing his neck. He forces out a breath. "The second you . . . " he forces in a small breath. He clutches against the grip of my hands. "The second you make a move . . . my people will . . . " He breathes in. " . . . stab you until you lie bleeding on the floor." He smiles as a small trickle of blood spurts from his mouth.

I rip the knife from my pocket and swing it as hard as I can against him. Within a second, everything is over . . . or maybe not.

That didn't feel like it went through!

I open my eyes against the tugging of a resistance. The man has caught the knife in his hands and is stopping it with the brute force of both his palms. I shudder in horror as he slowly pushes back the knife—both hands stabbed in the middle of the palm, his palms stacked together. He bites his lip and muffles some sound.

"You are going to die now, boy!"

"Stand down!" screams a voice from behind my shoulder. A hand pulls against my shoulder. I rip my shoulder and leverage my body upward. I push with my entire body weight as the man and I are in a sort of stalemate. Bit by bit, the man is pushing the knife away with all his strength.

"Sam!" screams Susan from the other side of the room. The man's green, bloodshot eyes flutter for a moment as he glances in Susan's direction. I quickly glance down at his plate, eye the butter knife on his tray, grab it in one motion, and swing upward with all the force I have.

The man stops moving—completely. Time slows and the room drops into a silence. A warm liquid seeps into the curvature of my hand. Blood begins streaming down my forearm and dripping off the sides of my arm to the ground below. I lean in and stare into his eyes. And then I say it: "One monster is plenty."

Within a second, two hands grasp my shoulders and attempt to rip me to the ground. As I stare up, my back is arched toward the ground. With everything I have, I reach up, clutch the knife, and dig it deeper into the soft mesh of the man's throat.

"*Uhhhh!*" My back slams against the ground as small black holes overtake pockets of my vision. A small amount of blood trickles into my mouth.

A boot kicks into my ribs. A large exhale of air pushes itself out of my lungs; I am breathless. Within moments, I am flipped onto my back with my hands pressing against the back side of my hips. Then, I am suddenly flipped face down. A click rings out as metal cuffs lock in place. A hand presses against the back of my neck—forcefully slamming me farther down, face down, into the linoleum floor. I feel nauseous. I feel nervous. I feel scared. *I feel . . . alive.* A brief smile creeps its way across my face. The hysteria of the moment overtakes me and I scream out in laughter. Blood seeps into my mouth, and I spit it out. I am chuckling, crying.

"Someone grab a first aid kit!" screams a voice from behind me. I tilt my head to the left. The mess hall is in a frenzy. A punch here, someone being tackled there. The sound of metal gates slamming in the distance. Food and trays are flying everywhere . . . tables are being flipped. *I've created a riot—my riot.*

An officer leans down, digging his knee into my back. "I knew it. I knew you were going to be a problem. You happy about what you've done?" I slowly turn my head to look up at him. Blood adheres to parts of my face and I just smile up at him. I am still laughing, somewhat manically. I look into his eyes and see terror.

"Welcome to our world," I say. "Sometimes, they deserve it."

The man I stabbed collapses on the floor and begins bleeding out. I look over at his body, now laying a couple of feet away. Several volunteers are gathered around him. "Sir, sir, can you hear me? Someone put pressure on his neck!" A small window appears through the legs of all the people. I lock eyes with him as he continues gargling blood. I watch as horror, terror, anguish, and probably many more emotions envelop his blood red face. I smile at him as I feel blood engross my two front teeth.

The mess hall is still in a frenzy. Screaming everywhere . . .

"Damnit, Susan! Call the police and get riot control down here!"

The knee digging into my back flies off. I look to my right. The officer pinning me against the floor slams into the floor. He immediately curls up and covers his bleeding face. I look up. Standing just to the right of me is another man. With both arms flexed he stares down at the security guard. "That is for not letting us stay here last week and shower!" The man then begins beating the security guard—kicking him in the face, ribs, and shoulder. After a few kicks, he drops on the man and begins slamming his hands on the back of the guard's head. The guard rolls up into a fetal position. I roll onto my back and press myself up and away from the floor. The man slams his hand into the crevice of the security guard's hands, immediately pulling him up. The man just laughs at the guard's bloodied and cut-up face. "Time to die, pig!"

The man reaches into his tattered green jacket and pulls out a makeshift shiv; part of the blade is serrated. The man grasps both hands around the knife and raises it. I look past the man holding the knife. The room is still in full riot.

One act of violence. That's all it took. One act and the shelter blew up in a frenzy of violence.

Save him. A voice rings out inside my head. *Save him.*

I shake my arms back and forth. *No use. I am stuck in these stupid cuffs.* I squirm my legs back and forth, arching my back in the process. With one large extertion of force, I kick outward with all of the tension in my legs.

I can feel the man's ribs depress as the force presses up and into my legs. I can feel the man's ribs crack under the pressure of my feet. The man launches off the ground and flies into the underside of the lunch tables; food flies off the table and rains down onto him. The man curls up instantly, wincing at the pain and exhaling forcefully. The security guard has a look of pure disbelief. One of his eyes, purple from all the hits, twitches back and forth.

A loud bang blasts out. An initial kick toward the back of the room—near the entrance to the shelter. Another kick echoes into the room. Police burst through the door. "Everyone on the ground! *Now!*"

Immediately the frenzy ends and everyone hits the floor, prone.

"You three: on the ground, now!" A squadron of policemen in riot uniforms enter the mess hall in an arrow formation. "I am not going to say it again. On the ground! *Now!*"

I look in the direction of the policemen. Three people are still standing. I look underneath one of the tables. Ol' Betty is one of them, alongside two other men. The looks on their faces are pure disgust.

"Last chance!" screams the officer at the point of the formation. I turn my attention back toward the monster I have stabbed. Two volunteers are pressing a bandage into his chin to try and stop the bleeding.

"We need help over here!" One of the volunteers pops his head above the cover of the tables, in the direction of the riot squadron. The policemen don't avert their gaze toward the volunteers. The front man keeps his gaze fixed on Betty.

"Get on the ground *now!*" screams the cop, once more, at the three of them.

"Fuck you!" Betty belts back. She grabs a lone tray from the table and hurls it at the cop as hard as she can. The tray flies across the room and grazes the side of the cop's face. The cop takes one step to the side. "I get jumped, rolled, mugged, and beat up all the time downtown. I think, 'Hey, maybe the police can help me,' because, you know, it's your fucking job! But no, we ain't worth your time, are we?" She extends her hands across the mess hall. "No, we ain't nothing to you. We don't pay your tax dollars, so you hate us!"

The cop pulls his gun and trains it on Betty. "Ma'am, I'm warning you. Get on the fucking ground or I will pull the trigger."

Betty stares at him even more intently. "Alright, officer. I am going to give you an incredible opportunity. Show these people you aren't what I say you are." The cop in the front cocks his hands and tightens them. "Fuck you!" Betty slowly opens her mouth as she snarls at him. She slings her arm into her pocket. The glimmer of a black object catches the incandescent light of the fixtures above us. Time seems to slow . . .

A loud gunshot echoes through the room. Back and forth it ricochets between the walls. Those on the ground cup their hands against their ears. A brief silence emerges. The silence is interrupted by the sound of a loud thump. I look over and see Betty's eyes glaring, but turned downward against the floor. Suddenly lifeless, her body begins to bleed out.

"You two! On the ground, *now!*" The cop screams at the two men who were standing behind Betty. Immediately, the men drop their chests to the floor.

No one is talking. Everyone just stares. The volunteers putting pressure against the man's neck peer at the police in shock. The cop tilts his head slightly and taps his communications radio. "We need multiple buses at the East Hills Shelter!"

The room remains quiet as the only sound is the police officers moving about. The security guard next to me rises to his feet; he is clenching his nose, halting the flow of blood. The security guard trudges over to the police sergeant. They converse for a couple of minutes and the security guard points at me. The police captain nods, mumbles into his radio for a moment, and then two officers quickly walk my way.

I shift my body weight; I have my head slightly raised from the ground. I place my forehead against the cold linoleum floor and take a deep breath in. In those manic few minutes, I had completely forgotten the cut on my face. Blood has soaked through the bandage and is nipping at the edge of the cut. A foul taste makes my mouth feel toxic. I spit blood onto the ground next to me. I lift my head slightly and look once again at the man I stabbed. The volunteers are still applying pressure. I look at the man's face; a ghostly white color has enveloped him. I take a deep breath and place my forehead back against the ground. My arms ache from the handcuffs.

The two officers approach me and forcefully lift me from the ground. While one officer places his hands on my cuffs and pushes them more tightly together, the other begins to speak. "You have the right to remain silent and to refuse to answer questions. Anything you say can or may be used against you in a court of law. You have the right to . . . "

The officer's words are drowned out as I scan the room. Everything appears as if in slow motion. Papers are in clusters falling to the floor; there are bouts of commotion from different spots around the room. I glance over at the front desk. Susan is frantically scanning the room. Everyone else stares in the direction of Betty as she lays in a pool of blood.

"Done?" says one of the officers.

"Yeah," confirms the officer on my left-hand side. Everything goes silent again.

A man ten feet away from me, still lying on the ground, slams his hand against the floor. *Clap!*

A woman two feet from him, on his left, slams her hand against the floor. *Clap!*

Two more people on the other side of the room join in. *Clap! Clap!*

A moment passes and ten more people join in. *Clap! Clap! Clap! Clap! Clap!* . . .

The claps fill the room. They echo off the floor and reverberate into the legs of the lunch tables. The trays vibrate and shake. Trays fall and slam to the floor.

"Alright. Take him!" screams the officer on my right. Forcefully, the first officer twists my body toward the front door while maintaining pressure against the cuffs on my back. As we are walking through the automatic doors, I turn my head back to the mess hall. The dessert boy who I attacked a few days earlier locks eyes with me. I smile at the boy; his face is in shock. Maybe incomprehension.

The officer jerks me through the front door. The sun hits the pavement outside—it is beating on my face. Besides that, something else is interesting. It's a gorgeous blue day. No clouds are looming over the shelter, no breeze sways the trees. There is nothing—just the blue of the sky and radiance of the sun. It is almost soothing. I sigh and let out a large breath. I can feel the anxiety from the situation slowly draining out of my face, into my neck, and finally dispersing from my body.

"Are you happy, Sam? Did you achieve what you came here to do? Are you excited . . . that this is the end?"

I quickly turn my head and peer over the head of the policeman escorting me out. It's Cam. Standing with his black ragged jacket, torn shoes, gray pants, and that rugged look on his face. Something, though . . . seems . . . off. Cam is completely shaven. The bulb of his head reflects the sun. His skin, where his beard was, is much lighter than the rest of his body. *Is Cam smaller?* Cam's body noticeably has seemed to shrink.

"Are you happy, Sam?" he demands again, his voice in monotone.

Blood is still dripping down my face and my hands tremble by my sides. The muscles in my face begin to twitch. Almost as if a surge of energy is taking over my face. A small smile morphs into a full-on grin. I can feel blood lace my front teeth, then fall onto my lower lip and drip off the center cusp.

Cam stands still. I can see his chest slowly moving with his breaths. He seems numb to the situation around him. Police are now swarming the area. Running in and out of the shelter. Cam seems impervious to all this bustle, however. His eyes remain fixed on me. He tilts his head toward the sky and stares. "You still haven't answered my question? Are you ready for the end?"

My feet become heavy as the distance between the police car and me seems to widen. *What does he mean by "the end"? There is no* end.

Finally, we're at the police car. As the officer opens the door, I continue to stare, in deadlock, with Cam. He slowly tilts his head down. Our eyes remain locked on each another. After what seems a very long time, he sighs heavily and then quickly turns his body and begins walking away from the shelter.

The officer jerks my head down and shoves me into the car. I immediately scan the back window, which is covered by metal bars. *No Cam.* Nothing. No sign of him anywhere. The spot where he began walking is now flooded with police officers. I turn my body back toward the front of the car and stare ahead.

"It was meant to be. It was meant to be. It was meant to be. It was meant to be." I chant these words in a rhythmic kind of mantra. The left front door of the police car opens and a large white man sits in the front seat and adjusts his mirrors.

"Guess where . . . "

"It was meant to be. It was meant to be. It was meant to be . . . " I continue to repeat this as I stare ahead, out the front window, toward the gleaming city in the distance. My face is flexed, firing. I can feel a grin now stretching from cheek to cheek. Blood is flowing down the side of my cheek and into my mouth. But I don't care. At all. "It was meant to be . . . " I just keep saying it.

"Shut your mouth or we are going to have a really big problem when we get to the station," shouts the officer in the driver's seat. The driver pulls out a small notepad from a pocket on his shirt, flips it open, pulls out a pen, and makes a few small scribbles. He then places the notepad back in his chest pocket.

I lean back against the seat and arch my back to conform to the rough surface. I close my eyes and quietly hum to myself. *I am the master of my fate, the captain of my soul* . . .

EIGHTEEN

THE BATMAN PARADOX

"Alright!" shouts the man as he makes his way into the room. He quickly turns his back and closes the door behind him. "How are we?" He slams his large brown leather briefcase onto the table and yanks a metal chair on the opposite side of the room toward the metal table. The chair's metal legs screech against the floor.

The man is short with black curly hair, a furrowed brow, and beads of sweat working their way along his sideburns. He is wearing a black suit with little fibers extending in each direction and a cheap blue tie with the label extending outward from the seam of the tie. His glasses push out from his face with a large brown frame and encompass most of his nose and eyes. His dialect rings out in something similar to what you might hear on an episode of *Friends*, where Joey uses the "How you doin?" tone. His facial hair, untamed and messy, looks as though it hasn't been trimmed or maintained in a week.

The man reaches for his briefcase, clicks the outside lock, and it flies open with a flurry of papers. "Damn it, Stacy, I told you to please"—he enunciates, and motions with his fingers—"*please* put my legal papers in order and then in a paper clip! It's not like I asked five freaking times already!"

The papers fly out of his briefcase and around the room. A couple this way, a couple that, a mirage of legal documents floating around. "Son of a bitch!" the man exhales sharply, slamming his hands on his pant legs.

I look on as he lets out another large sigh and rises to his feet. The man mumbles to himself as he walks to each side of the room and collects the papers—now all completely wrinkled. "I should fire her," he mutters.

This goes on for a solid minute. Some papers fall from his hand, then he retraces his steps and grabs the same papers again. Bit by bit, the papers all get collected in a jumbled mess. He walks back to the table, slams the papers down, and pulls out his chair. He plops himself down and sighs intensely.

He clenches the skin between his eyebrows as he places his elbows against the table. Finally, he reaches for the pile and slowly moves through individual pieces, carefully looking for and placing some in a pile on his lap. After about two more minutes, a stack of about forty pages sits on his lap in a jumbled, unorganized mess. Every few papers brings a murmured "son of a bitch." The end of each word slurs off partially—probably a lisp.

"OK," he shouts out as the back of my spine curls and I jump slightly from my seat. "Sam Case! My name is Isaac Adler. Pleasure to make your acquaintance." He rips his hand out from under the desk and shoots it in my direction; I flinch from the sudden movement. His hand appears sweaty and clammy from all the paper sorting.

I swallow. "Um, Sam Case." I reach for his hand, but he suddenly pulls it back.

"But of course, you already knew that I was Isaac Adler. And I of course know who you are, because you are my client and I am your legal counsel. I am the public defender for you and all you other hoodlums who do stupid shit. Excuse me for a moment." He reaches into his coat pocket and yanks out a large handkerchief. One moment perfectly normal, the next he is violently coughing and sneezing into the handkerchief. He motions the cloth in my direction. "Do you need to use it?"

I just shake my head.

"Alrighty, then!" He shoves the messy handkerchief back into his pocket and corrects the alignment of his coat. His dress is a mess; his coat jacket looks like the buttons are about to fall off their threads. His jacket is still askew.

"Um, you should fix your blazer?" I say, softly, as I point to it.

"What's that?" he says as he looks downward. "Oh, that. Thank you." He adjusts the blazer. In short, he is a total slob.

My jaw hangs in disgust as I stare.

"OK!" he belts out again, nearly making me fall from my seat. "Where were we?" He trifles with the papers in his lap, looking up at me as if I am going to give him a serious answer.

"Um, I'm Sam Case. And you're my lawyer," I mutter, the words stumbling out.

"Right," he says as he throws a piece of paper on the table. "So, just so we're clear, I am going to go over what has happened the past week or so, so you understand what has happened, because I am pretty sure you're just as dumbfounded as the rest of the people that have sat in your chair."

I nod slowly, in confusion.

"OK!" He raises his voice again. *His tone is becoming so annoying.* He raises his arm sleeve to his face and brushes it against his nose. *This guy is disgusting. Is this guy for real?*

He straightens the papers again. He pulls them to his face as his eyes squint under his large glasses. "Following your arrest at the East Hills homeless shelter, you were brought here to Alameda Police Station. At which point you were booked—your background, picture, yada yada yada. Following booking, you chilled in the police station jail for three days."

"Not 'chilled.' Waited for you to hurry up and visit."

He looks up from the paper, just enough to where the underside of his eyes are cut off by the presence of the paper. "You *chilled*," he barks back. "Now shut up. I am explaining lawyering."

He whips his eyes back toward the paper. "During your chilling period"—he sarcastically makes quotation symbols with his hands—"evidence as to your conviction was presented in front of a grand jury with multiple witnesses. In accordance with the events at time of the murder"—he motions with his fingers to make quotations again—"there were a total of seventy-six witnesses who observed the event.

"For real? You couldn't pick a more secluded placed to kill this guy? You had to do it in the middle of a freaking crowd? The gall of some." He readjusts his glasses, pressing them even tighter to his face. "Anyway, Mister Public Enemy," he says sarcastically, pulling the paper down to catch my eyes. "And that's you—if you're not catching my drift."

I sigh and shrug. "Yes, I get that now. Please get with it. This may be fun for you, but I am sick of sitting in this hot-ass room!"

"Shut up and let me finish," he spews.

I roll my eyes as he pulls the paper close to his face again. "Anyway, back to where we were: there were a total of seventy-six witnesses. Of these witnesses, only six were deemed viable by the grand jury. These included the security guard, who said, quote, 'He saved my life.'" Adler uses a mocking, heroic tone. He peers over the paper. "Good job, superman." He lowers his eyes again. "Others included the secretary, two more security guards, and some of the people working the food service line that day."

"Was that boy, the one working the line that day, one of the people to provide testimony?" I ask, leaning forward in my seat.

Adler just smiles. "Yep . . . not going to tell you that." He smirks.

"Anyway!" he shouts, once again. "So many damn interruptions." I roll my eyes. "The piece of paper that you signed post-arrest—the information act—was presented in accordance with any relevant evidence to the grand jury. Alongside the evidence provided and the substantial amount of witness testimony, you were indicted on one count of murder in the first degree. It was then following that indictment that you met with a judge at the circuit court for your personal arraignment. At said arraignment you were notified of your rights: the right to counsel, a speedy trial, security without persecution—yada, yada, yada. I am not going to reiterate the same things they told you yesterday. And that brings us to now!" He slams a piece of paper on the table and glares at me. "The judge should have notified you that you are unable to post bail due to the punitive measures of your indictment. Any questions?"

I just stare at him, my teeth grinding inside my mouth.

"Why the stern look, kid? I am here to help you." He stares again at the pile of papers now sitting to his side. "Anyway, here is what's to come. We will have status hearings in court until a decision has been agreed upon between the judge, the DA, or deputy DA—it's probably going to be that asshole Derek," he whispers under his breath. "Anyway. We will have status court hearings until you plead guilty on account of your indictment—in which case we can negotiate a plea bargain."

"I . . ."

"So!" he interrupts loudly, drowning me out. "Let me tell you what you should do—actually I have to say what *I* think you should do, since I am your court-appointed attorney. You . . ."

"I . . ."

"You . . . should consider the possibility—more like eventuality . . . of pleading guilty. There were so many witnesses and testimony that it would be hard to negotiate a reasonable plea bargain if we fight. If you do plead guilty, we could negotiate for minimal sentencing, due to a first-time offense, and we could possibly work out some conditions with the judge to keep you out of gen pop."

"Gen pop?" All I can do is ask what the heck that means.

"Yeah." His voice is shrill again. "You know. Gen pop stands for general population. Come on, kid. Keep up! That way you aren't with all those psychos and rapists who just want to get at your goodies."

I stare in horror.

"Ahh, it's not that bad," he says. "If we do get this deal, then we can try and negotiate a private cell for the entirety of your sentence. Wouldn't that be nice! What do you say?"

I remain silent as he looks me up and down. After a moment of silence, he motions his hands to the side in a theatrical way.

"Uh, kid. You're making this harder than it needs to be. How about this: I'll walk you through it . . . again." His tone is mocking. "Do you fully understand the criminality of your actions and do you believe that you have committed wrongdoing? That is one of the first things that I learned in law school, and it is the basis for the legality of the system."

I remain silent, my hands crossed.

"Ugh, kid. Come on!" He presses his fingers against the wrinkle between his eyebrows and moves them up and down. "Kid, do you understand the criminality of your actions? Or, to put it in a lighter frame: do you believe that you did something wrong by killing the man? By the way, before you answer, a lot of people, hopefully all of them"—he states as he maneuvers his torso rotationally across the room—"would say yes to that statement. Preschool taught you . . . hopefully . . . it is wrong to kill someone. The Bible also says, 'It is wrong to kill someone.'" He seems to make some sort of strange religious praying motion and sound as he delivers that last line. "Besides, you are a smart kid. I've seen your academic file. You know exactly what I'm talking about."

I remain silent and continue to cross my arms. I clamp my fingers to my arms and squeeze. I bite the inside of my cheek on the left-hand side to relieve some of the pain that has built up alongside my cheek cut.

"Well, actually, no," he interjects. "Let's just sit here and let the drama build as if we were in some book or movie or something. I'll wait." Adler leans back in his chair and begins to hum the theme song for *Law and Order.*

I grind the back of my teeth as he begins to hum louder and louder, and is now incorporating various parts of his body for theatrical effect. Adler looks up at the ceiling and closes his eyes. With each passing second, he gets louder and louder.

"Dun, dun!" he screams out at the end of the song. At this point, I'm seeing Adler as a total weirdo. *This is my lawyer?*

"Alright, kid. You're trying my patience. I am going to get up and leave and you are going to be stuck in that cell for another night as I come up with some weird lawyer shit to try and make you talk. For both of our sakes, let's skip that part and you just answer my damn question."

"I . . ."

Adler leans forward and twists his head, purposely turning his right ear toward me.

"I . . . killed that man because he deserved to die. I don't think I should be punished by any means for taking care of"—and here, I motion my fingers in quotations—"someone that so clearly deserved to die."

"Oh fuck," sighs Adler as he buries his face in his hands and leans back in the chair. He pulls down on his eyelids, then his nose, and then finally his mouth and chin. He yanks the pile of papers closer. He slowly begins sorting through the stack of papers again.

"I always get these ones . . . damn it, Stacy," he murmurs as he sorts through the papers. "Ahh, here it is." His voice is finally lower for once.

"OK. The man that you killed was named Peter A. Savage. He had an extensive criminal record. He served five years when he was 16 for breaking and entering. Another ten years when he was 26 for possession of illegal substances and child pornography. And finally, he was detained in the drunk tank for the night last year when he was found stumbling down the streets and harassing children and teenagers as they entered the mall. He was 47 at the time of his death. The coroner's report"—he places one piece of paper back on the table and reaches for another; he now lays his finger on that page—" . . . the coroner's report claimed that the cause of death was from a laceration to something called 'the left internal carotid artery.' As to the object of usage . . . . a . . . butter knife! Holy shit, you used a butter knife to kill this guy? I knew it was a knife, but I didn't know it was a butter knife. That's hardcore!" Adler looks up from the paper in amazement.

He sighs and looks again at the paper. "Alright, anyway. The coroner's report states that one branch of the internal carotid artery was severed and he died of internal bleeding."

The hairs on my arms stand up and I can feel the beating of my heart get more and more intense. I can't help but deliver a partial smile.

Adler gazes up at me. "Damn, are you smiling? That's messed up! Anyway, back to my earlier question. You feel you have committed no wrongdoing because this guy was what you consider to be 'scum,' or a bad person."

I nod. "Finally, we agree on something," I say quietly but sternly.

Adler smudges his fingers against the wrinkle folds on his forehead and massages each groove. "So, what you are basically telling me is that you are not fit to stand trial?" His eyebrows move upward, skeptically.

"I don't know what that means."

"Fit," he articulates, using quotations, gesturing again. "Or 'fitness,' as it is known in the legal definition. Being 'fit' to stand trial is someone who is not able to aid in their own legal defense either by means of a mental defect in compliance with state statutes or those defined as one not able to appreciate the criminality of their actions through means of compliance." He places his hands on his lap and rubs them. His face is flustered and his complexion dampens into a flush of red.

"I don't really understand what that means in any regard. But if it's what I think it is, it's that you think I don't understand exactly what I have done." I point to my chest, my heart. "That I don't understand the wrongdoing in the act I have committed."

Isaac corrects the position of his back against the metal chair and bolts upright even while still seated. "Exactly! That is exactly what I am trying to tell you!" His voice is raised.

I remain very calm.

"What I did by killing that man is by no means wrong. I shouldn't be punished for killing someone that truly was evil and doesn't deserve to live by any means. He targeted people to molest them. He stalked me to the point in which I thought I was going to die up on a roof. He raped me! He was never going to leave me alone! And if not me, then someone else. I saw the way he looked at the boy in line. I see the way he looks at the younger people at the shelter. I killed him because it was my right. It was something I was meant to do!" My voice is raising with each word. Pressure builds under the skin of my face and swells toward my cut. I grind the back of my front teeth and stare, bloodshot, at the lawyer. He sits in a stupor. No notetaking, this time no scattering of papers, just complete flabbergast. "He deserved to die!" With that, I slam my hand on the table.

Isaac jumps on impact. He has a look of terror. The chair behind me flies back and slams against the floor with a metallic ring. My hands remain cuffed to a small notch in the table as I stand.

The door to the room swings open. Two officers, one with his shoulder lowered and another with his hand latched to his belt, make their way in.

"Wait!" screams Adler, turning to the officer. "Everything is fine. Everything is fine. My client was simply exhibiting disgust as to the legality of his indictment. Please, everyone. Please remain calm."

The officers freeze in place as they stare at me. Adler calmly and slowly brushes some fibers off his coat, rises to his feet, and turns toward the officers. "Officers, I apologize for my client's outburst. If you would be so kind as to let us continue our defense preparation, I would greatly appreciate it."

The officers' postures loosen. "If you say so," declares the one on the right. "But if we hear another outburst, we are taking him back to his cell, and this will have to wait for another day."

Adler nods in agreement. "Of course, sir. I can promise that my client will not have another outburst again. Isn't that so, Sam?" he says, looking back my way and motioning for me to make a response.

My whole face is tense. I can feel each pulse of my heart run through the veins pressed against the tissue in my face.

"Good," Adler rings out, turning back to the officers. "Now if you would so kind as to let us continue?"

They glance at each other and retreat toward the door. Both look back one more time as they exit. Isaac—suddenly, in my mind, I am beginning to think of him as Isaac, not Adler—brushes more of the loose fibers that are collecting on his pants from his blazer. He walks around the table and behind me, slowly picks up the chair, and drags it back until it touches the back of my knees. The sound screeches and echoes against the tile floor.

I grimace at the sound as Isaac's face remains unchanged. He has a slight look or worry, but remains cold.

"If you would be so kind as to sit." Isaac motions toward the chair.

I glare at him. My face is still flush from excitement and my legs jolt with an influx of adrenaline. I slowly sink back into the chair. My heart pounds against my ribs. Each exhale pulses down my face and into my spine.

"Alright," murmurs Isaac in a quiet, concerted tone. "Now that that distraction is out of the way, we need to get something straight." He pulls the chair out from the opposite side of the table and slowly lowers himself into it. He reaches for the pile of papers on his left-hand side, licks his finger, and carefully looks at each paper, one by one. "Ahh, here we are."

"What exactly needs to be made straight?" I ask.

"This is your toxicology report taken after you were arrested. Do you remember that?"

I nod; I certainly remember the test.

"OK. Well, your toxicology report says that at the time you carried out the crime, you had no foreign substances in your system—none." He motions his hand parallel across the table. "So that means that you were in a physiologically right state of mind."

I nod again, slowly. But I'm unsure what he is getting at.

"I will file on behalf of your defense and let the DA's office and the court know that we are filing for a full psych evaluation. At this juncture, it is clear to me that you don't appreciate the criminality of your actions. The public defender's office will personally hire a forensic psychologist to evaluate, and I am sure the state will also want to hire one."

I blink slowly and twist my eyebrow. "So, let me get this straight." I lean in. "I may be young, but I am by no means stupid. You believe me to be insane or at least in some respect to have a mental deficiency because I believe that my actions are justified, and I don't think I should be punished?"

He continues looking through the papers. He's glancing up and down with a disappointed look on his face. His eyes briefly spark and he places three pages on the table while moving the remaining stack down the table. He takes a deep breath and looks up from the table. "Yes, that is exactly what I am saying. My role here is to provide you with legal defense in a manner in which we can both create the best possible future scenario for you. As of this moment, it seems you are unfit to aid in your own legal defense. But there is one thing I want to check before I leave, and then I'll bring in the evaluation tomorrow for you to sign."

"And what might that be?" I just stare at the papers on the table.

"In front of me here . . . " he says as he motions across the three papers. " . . . are some scenarios that I would like you to consider. But before I get into that, I want to ask you a question."

"OK." I'm baffled.

"To you, Sam, is Batman the hero of the comics—or is he the villain?"

Stupefied by this question, my eyebrows shoot up. "I am pretty sure that most people would probably say he is the hero. He does what it takes to stop the villains of Gotham from inflicting harm on others."

"Right you are," he says as he motions with a point of his finger. "But have you ever heard the theory that maybe the acts he is committing, the sort of vigilantism he carries out, impedes the justice system, because he believes his actions to be justified due to a singular incident?"

I stare in bewilderment.

"See, to the observer, it looks as though Batman is doing something he believes is justified to save others. He believes he is carrying out an act for the betterment of humanity. But within the realm of the law, he is taking the law into his own hands and exerting his will on people for what is considered 'a lack of evidence.'"

I tighten my back and lean closer to the table. "I don't know exactly where you are going with this, but if I am going to play along, he is saving them before they know they need to be saved."

"Exactly! And isn't that exactly what you are doing?" He glances down at the papers. "Or, let's say someone else was investigating your indictment through the lens of objectivity. Some may question that it is an act of vengeance or an act of some ulterior force."

"Ulterior force? I don't know what you mean." I lean back and bite the bottom of my lip.

"The three documents I have on the table are your medical records from your visit to the hospital, records from the shelter staff, and finally, records and observations collected from the site of the arrest as well as the booking notes."

"OK. Please, get on with it!"

He motions for calm and reaches for the paper on his left. "When you were brought into the hospital, the notes from the medical staff were limited. They said, 'The patient is unresponsive about the events leading to his arrival.' But what the notes lacked in subjective analysis, they made up for in medical documentation. 'The patient, Samuel Case, arrived with a large laceration to his right cheek, a mild grade concussion, and several signs of rape/molestation."

Isaac looks at me with curiosity. He tilts his head to the side briefly and then lifts the paper closer to his face. "'The signs of sexual molestation seemed fresh, with various contusions."

I grind my front teeth more tightly.

"Let me ask you one more question." Isaac clasps his hands. "Is it possible—and the DA will probably come to this same conclusion—that the act you committed was not one for the betterment of humanity, but an act of revenge? My guess—and again, I am on your side of this debate, but I need to make sure—is that you wanted to kill him *not* because he raped, molested, and hurt you."

My heart pounds and presses against my ribs; my face is flush with adrenaline. I violently push myself out of my seat. The chair under my body flies back again, this time with enough force to slam against the wall. "I killed him because he deserved to be killed!" I scream. My voice echoes around the room. The door handle vibrates back and forth. "It does look like I killed him out of revenge. But let me tell you this! . . . "

Isaac just remains seated and stares intently—this time, there is no look of anxiety about him. His body is relaxed and poised. The door into the room swings open and slams against the wall. The officers rush in as I flex my arms and pull tightly against the chain. "I killed him because he was going to do it again! The same thing was going to happen to another person because he was never going to change. You saw his criminal record. I know it's in that shitty little stack of papers. I know it is!"

The guards rush at me. While one pushes me against the table, the other removes my cuffs from the notch. The first presses my face down into the cold table. Blood begins oozing into my mouth from the impact.

I stare at Isaac—still sitting in his chair calmly. One of my eyes is closed shut from the force of the officer's hand. "I have done nothing wrong! Nothing wrong in the slightest," I gargle in a sort of scream as the officers jerk me toward the door. My back is now turned away from Isaac as the light from the hallway slithers into the room. I am yelling as they push me through the room and toward the door. "I don't appreciate the criminality of my actions because I have done nothing criminal!"

The officers shove me into the hallway. I kick my feet to try and stop them. The door behind me slams shut and echoes around the surrounding hallway.

NINETEEN

PSYCHOSIS

"Sam Case?"

I sit up from the cold metal bench supposedly called a bed. "Yeah?"

"A doctor from Green Belt Psychiatry is here to evaluate you. Let's go," says the officer as he motions down the cellblock; a large buzzer rings out. The prison bars swing open to the left and the officer steps into the cell.

"Against the wall!" says the officer as he points. I sigh and place my head against the cold concrete wall and breathe out heavily. The officer cautiously approaches me and nudges my feet farther apart. Quickly, he places my hands behind my back. He cuffs them together and removes my head from the wall. I look down at my feet. The blue prison slippers are horrible. Absolutely no comfort, no support, and I can feel the cold concrete below me with each step. They pale in comparison to the white color of the prison-style jumpsuit I'm wearing. I might as well be naked. Every night since the first day in prison, I have been asking the prison guard to find me an extra blanket. I didn't realize freezing to death is a part of my punishment.

The officer whips my body toward the opening of the cell and pushes me sternly from the middle of my back into the hall. I look both ways down the hall: one way leads to a dead end with a small barred window covered with hazed glass, and the other way leads to a barred door. A small trickle of light seeps in through the barred window on the left side. I reach out with my hands. The officer shoves me in the back. "No funny business, Case." The officer then turns me away, toward the barred door. "Behave, and you won't get shoved in the back anymore." The officer presses me forward, then squeezes my arm to halt my momentum. The officer behind me bellows out: "Prisoner 2314: leaving cellblock."

Another officer behind the barred door motions to his right, down another hallway. Another large buzzing sound rings out as the electronic lock for the door slides inward. The officer on the other side approaches the barred entrance, pivots the clutch lever, and the door swings open. "Hey Bradley, what room is Case in today?" asks the officer escorting me.

A sound echoes from the speaker above. "He's in Room 4. Dr. Hypatia is waiting for him."

"Oh, Dr. Hypatia. Sounds good," says the officer behind me. "Let's go," he says. I look down the hall to where the officer who opened the door was standing. Just right, down the hall, is a bulletproof glass room with a small ring of holes. Inside, a man in a correctional officer uniform is staring intensely at a TV monitor.

The officer presses me forward. "No time for lollygagging, Case." We begin walking down the hall. Along the right side of the hall are sequential windows, about two feet wide and high, with bars covering them, similar to the small window at the end of the hall outside my cell. These windows, however, are clear and show the outside world. It's a gorgeous day. The sun shines brightly into the surrounding greenscape of the city. I look out one of the windows. The trees are slowly beginning to brown as the change of seasons approaches. I take a deep breath. The smell of fresh air slows my heart for a moment. My body loosens and relaxes at the sight of the sky. I close my eyes and . . .

"Come on!" says the officer as he continues to push me down the hall. We walk another twenty feet. "Stop here," he says as he tightly grips my arm. "Alright. Room 4." Another officer is standing outside the door and nods as we approach. He reaches for the door and quickly opens it. As we round the corner, I peer inside. There sits a woman in a red, tight shirt and black pants with black styled heels. She's at the lone table in the room, which is silver metal and contrasts with the bleak white of the rest of room.

The officers push me forward to the other side of the room. "Turn around," says one, and both position themselves beside me.

I nod slightly and stare at the linoleum tiles covering the floor. "Nothing funny here, Case." The officer on my left side places his hand on my shoulder while the other officer swings around to my backside and uncuffs me. "Turn around," says the officer behind me. I cautiously turn my body toward the table. Both officers place their hands on my shoulders and push down. My knees give out and I collapse into a chair below. "Alright, now hands on the table," both say, nearly in unison. I lift my uncuffed hands in the air. Both officers clutch at my shoulders as I wince from the pressure. "Ow!" I belt out.

"Just hurry up, Case."

I place both hands on the metal table. "Flip them around with the palms facing the ceiling," one of them says.

I do this, and the officer on my right leans across the table. He slips the cuffs through the small carabiner in the table.

I stare in the direction of the woman who must be Dr. Hypatia. She is studying numerous files on the table. The officers recuff me and place my hands back on the table. I pull slightly against the chains. *Very tight on both sides. I hate these stupid things.* The officers step back into the corners of the room and stand still.

Dr. Hypatia licks her fingers as she paces quickly through her notes. She looks up at times, staring at me diligently. Her brunette eyebrows raise against the slight indentations on her forehead. She brushes her hair to the side of her face and pushes it behind her ears.

"Oh, gentlemen, I understand it is protocol to stay in the room with me, but as you know, he is restrained," she says to the officers. "I feel as though people undergoing psychiatric evaluation open up more if there is no authoritative figure in the room. Would it be alright if you left the room until I have concluded the evaluation?"

I turn back to look at one of the officers and offer him a smile. The officers look at each other briefly, then shrug. The one in the left corner of the room appears to swallow. "Of course, ma'am," he says. "If you need us we will be right outside the door. Just knock when you're done." His disappointed tone says it all. These officers love this lady. They step toward the door as I wave at them—yes, sarcastically.

"Thank you, gentlemen," she says, smiling and continuing to examine her notes.

The two officers exit; one actually looks jealous. The other simply stares at me for the last few seconds as the door closes.

Dr. Hypatia continues sifting through her notes. A brief period passes. The clock in the room hums out each second as I let out a large breath. "Um, excuse me," I say—but she cuts me off.

She quickly points up with her finger, motioning for me to remain silent. She lowers her glasses on her face and collects the pile of notes in an orderly fashion. She drops her glasses with a clank against the hard, cold surface of the table.

"Alright!" she says, and sternly. She places a Dictaphone on the table and presses the red button.

"OK, please state your name for the record," she says, looking at me directly.

"Umm . . . Samuel Case," I mutter.

"Would you prefer me to call you Samuel or Sam for the sake of this evaluation?" She pulls out a yellow notepad and removes a pen from her binder. She gazes at me as though genuinely curious.

"Sam is fine," I reply.

"OK, Sam. I want to introduce myself. My name is Dr. Hannah Hypatia. I am a forensic psychologist with the Green Belt Psychiatric Institute. I have been assigned to your case on behalf of the United States and the state of Washington. If you have any questions during the evaluation, please feel free to ask."

I nod.

"Alright, let's begin." She seems poised with her pen lifted above paper. "What kind of person would you say you are?" she asks, cocking her head.

"Umm, what?" My eyebrows curve inward.

"What kind of person do you see yourself as? Meaning, if you were to describe yourself, what details would you list?"

I place my hands in my lap and twiddle my thumbs. I swallow. "What does that have to do with anything?"

"Please answer the question," she says, sounding impatient. She peers up from her notes and folds her hands. "It helps me get a better grasp of who you are and allows me to generate a baseline. Now if you would, please."

I nod, confused as to how she could possibly establish a reliable baseline from a single question. "Alright, I . . . uh . . . I would say that I am a person who . . . " And then, nothing—no typifying trait comes to mind when I think of myself. I close my eyes and watch images float by, one after the other. Finally: "I would say I am a person who survives."

"And what exactly does that entail?" I see that she is writing "Survivor" in large letters.

"It . . . it means that I will fight through anything." I say it bold and stern. "It means that no matter what happens to me, no matter the scenario or situation or problem, I will always come out on the other side."

"Interesting," she replies as she begins to make notes. "What else?"

I shake my head. I don't think I have anything else to add.

"OK, to add further to what I said earlier, my role here is to evaluate your ability to aid in your own legal defense. Based on my legal notes, it says that you 'indirectly'"—she puts emphasis on the word—"asked for an evaluation. Would you please explain the indirect part to me?"

I nod; I'll seek to comply. "I stated to my attorney that I don't believe there is any criminal element to my actions. When questioned if I understood the criminality of my actions, I stated that I didn't believe my actions were 'clearly criminal.' In fact, it is the opposite. I believe that my actions are justified and, by every means, that man deserved to die."

"But you do understand that you have committed an action that is considered wrong in the eyes of society, the law, and subjective morality?" She is fidgeting with her fingers and the pen as it swings back and forth against the legal pad below.

"I do not."

"Interesting," she replies. She lowers her head and scribbles something.

"Alright. Now that we have that out of the way, why don't we start at the beginning? What I want you to do now is to recreate the scenario of the killing prior to it occurring. Let's say . . . talk about the previous day, and work your way up to the events as they unfolded. And if an emotion was prominent during a certain action—please elaborate."

I move my arms upward even while sitting in the chair. The chains clank against each other and ring out as they ricochet off the metal.

"Mr. Case? If you will?" Hypatia says as she arches her elbow, ready to begin writing.

I take a deep breath and swallow hard. I feel a pit in my throat as I try to fight it downward. I shudder and breathe out.

"Ma'am, if you would be so kind as to not take notes, that might help a lot. I get anxiety when I see people writing something on my behalf. Even if it is a doctor or something else."

Dr. Hypatia looks down at her notepad and then over to the Dictaphone. She looks back and forth for a moment and then simply nods her agreement. She reaches for the Dictaphone, lifts it off the table, and places it more in the center of the table—just out of the reach of my hands. She moves her notepad to the side. Moving everything out of the way, she looks forward.

She extends her hand in a swift motion. "If you would, please!" She smiles and then just watches me.

"Alright. Well, I guess the best place to start would be when Cam and I were walking from the West Valley River Shelter toward the East Hills Shelter. We had spent the night at the West Valley River Shelter and Cam had woken me up early that morning so we could get to the East Hills Shelter for lunch. Monday is Salisbury steak day, and that just happens to be Cam's favorite lunch, so of course I had to get up earlier and walk ten miles across town. Literally. Just so Cam could have his stupid steak." I look at Dr. Hypatia. She has a look of bewilderment on her face.

She reaches for the stack of folders she has laid out across the table.

"Continue," she utters as she searches through the files. She places a file titled "Shelter Personnel and Records" in front of her.

"Umm, alright. Well, anyway, Cam and I walked across town all morning in hopes of getting to the East Hills Shelter. Cam and I got into a disagreement and we started arguing. I was exhausted and wanted to take a break, but Cam was worried that if we waited too long we would end up at the very back of the line. We ended up getting into a huge fight and it delayed our arrival, so as you can imagine, Cam was pretty upset."

"Excuse me," Dr. Hypatia says as she scans the file in front of her. "I am looking at the shelter personnel files here, and I can't find anyone under the name of Cam, or Cameron, for that matter. Do you by chance know his last name or if he uses a different name?"

I lift my head and gaze at the ceiling. I close my eyes for a moment. *I can't remember if Cam went by another name. Every time I was with him, he just said, "Call me Cam."*

"You know what?" My eyes are cast up at the ceiling as I respond. "I don't think I ever learned Cam's last name. I always just called him Cam—or dipshit." I chuckle to myself as I continue probing my memory. I open my eyes and gaze at Dr. Hypatia. The expression on her face is unchanged.

"Can you please describe him for me?" She pulls the legal pad and pen out to . . . once again start taking notes.

I look at her with some dismay. "I thought you said you weren't going to take notes?"

"Yes, I did. And I apologize for pulling out my notes, but I can't find any record of this man anywhere in the personnel file. He must go by another name, so I want to cross-check the description of this man with some of the evidence of discovery and testimony of others." She lowers her head and, with dexterity, poses the pen at an awkward angle. "Now, if you would please describe him?"

Dr. Hypatia readjusts her glasses, pushing them closer to her face. She contorts her knees, placing one on top of the other. She presses the pen socket and it clicks. She looks up, lifting her eyebrows. 'Whenever you are ready."

"Um, yeah, sure. Cam is a taller man, about six-foot-four."

"His ethnicity? The color of his skin?"

"Oh, umm, he is black. I would say African-American. He never really told me where he was from or anything about his family. Most people on the streets don't like discussing their upbringings, so I just ignored it. But yeah, I would say that he is a tall, scruffy-looking black man."

"Alright, please continue." She is feverishly scribbling notes at this point.

"Alright, so as I was saying, he is tall, maybe six-four. He is really scruffy-looking, until I saw him the other day, and he was cleanly shaven on both his head and his beard. He usually wears a green jacket as well as his dog tags around his neck. He is always wearing black pants with multiple pockets and black combat boots—which he laces about four thousand times back and forth." I chuckle as a smile creeps across my face. This image of Cam captures my mind's eye. I can see him standing on the corner asking for money—usually to no avail.

"OK, is there anything else that comes to mind when thinking about this Cam?" Dr. Hypatia hasn't looked up from her notepad for two or three minutes. She frantically records words as quickly as they fall from my mouth.

"Um, no ma'am. I don't believe so. I never really asked that much about his past or who exactly he was or where he came from. He was just someone who was always there for me. If I was ever in a bind, he was usually one to show up and help." A tension seems to grip the room. Dr. Hypatia's friendly, calm demeanor is changing. Smiling in the beginning, now she is intent on capturing every word.

Then she drops her pen on the table. The pen rolls back and forth, side to side, and slowly comes to a stop. She looks up from the notepad, smiles briefly, and then tucks the pad back into her mound of folders. "I will have to cross-check this information with a couple of things to see if this Cam can help in character testimony for the court or aid in the legal process. He may be someone who can help exonerate you in this case. I will tell the public defender about this as well."

"Umm, OK," I say, almost stuttering.

"Anyway, I apologize for interrupting. Please, continue with your story, Sam." She hums as she moves her legs back to a normal position and then leans forward in her chair.

"Yes, ma'am," I answer. "Well, following our arrival at the homeless shelter, I got into a scuffle with one of the boys serving in the food service line."

"Why is that?"

I cup my right arm with my left hand and slowly move the left hand back and forth, rubbing the elevated scar that ranges from my wrist to a point about three-fourths of the way up my arm. "Umm . . . "

"No need to worry, Sam. I just need to know for the record." Dr. Hypatia averts her gaze from my eyes down to my arm. She watches intently as I rub back and forth. Initially, cautiously, and then with more determination, she asks, "Does it have something to do with your arm?"

"Uh, yeah. The night my mom died . . . " My heart starts beating faster as my stomach starts to ache from the pressure. My arm begins burning and I can't seem to control the rate at which I rub up and down my arm. "The night my . . . " Faster and faster it swells. My pulse feels like it is compounding, squeezing at my air tract and drying up my mouth. The air feels heavier as each breath weighs on my lungs. I rub faster and faster. Back and forth, back and forth.

"Sam?" Dr. Hypatia interjects. She is now leaning over the table and gripping my left arm to hold it still. "I read the file of your family history. I know about that night. It's alright if you want to exclude that from your story."

I start to breathe more slowly. I nod in agreement.

"You were at 'a scuffle broke out,'" Dr. Hypatia says as she motions for me to continue.

"Uh, yeah. I was standing in line for the food service and the kid looked at me wrong and I just exploded. I lunged over the dessert cart and gripped him by his collar. I could see out of the corner of my eyes that everyone was reaching for something in their pockets. Security saw me do this, along with everyone else in the line. Security came over, grabbed me, and put me on the floor. The kid and his mom, who also happened to be working there that day, decided not to press charges."

"Where was Cam during this whole event?" Dr. Hypatia asks. She is twirling her fingers while she awaits my answer.

I peer to the side of the room, feeling like I'm in a bit of a quasi-trance.

I wrack my brain—any bit of information will be helpful. "I actually don't know where Cam went. He was in line when we got there. I was talking to the lady at the reception desk and then I lost track of him. I figured he had simply gone to the bathroom or up to the locker room to wash his face. Never really asked, I guess."

"Interesting," murmurs Dr. Hypatia as she looks on. Something I said seems to have piqued her interest. Every few words, it looks as though she is retreating into the back of her brain—calculating various bits of information. Again, she extends her hands to motion for me to continue.

"Anyway, security let me go, and I went to go sit at a bench in the back of the room. Everyone looked on edge, so I tried to remove myself from the situation. I ate as quickly as I could. I didn't want to attract any more attention to myself. Right before I was about to leave, I remember Cam saying that we should grab some bread for the road just in case we got hungry later on. I walked up to the bread cart—and he was there." I shudder at the thought. An image of Savage.

"I am assuming you mean Mr. Savage," Hypatia inquires.

I nod slowly, sternly, sadly.

"His breath smelled so bad I just wanted to vomit. But he told me I was in the wrong for making a scene. I just wanted to get away so bad. Cam was outside waiting for me. We both decided that it would probably be a good idea to grab some money—for us, that's panhandling—so we split up so we could try and get more. I went to the spot where I've had the most success in the past. You know, the spot right off the freeway, where it's a five-way road?"

Dr. Hypatia nods, slowly, her eyes moving upward as though thinking.

"Well, when I got there, Mr. P, a guy who frequents the shelters, was there as well. I wasn't having any luck panhandling, so Mr. P shows me some of the things he does to get money. He hands me his sign, which said, 'Smile,' and I tried to do the things he showed me. As I stood there, I could just feel everyone laughing and saying things about me. I felt as though I was going mad. I didn't want to be stared at anymore, so I just . . . ran."

"Very interesting," Dr. Hypatia says, and this time her voice seems more reassuring. The more I talk, the more I notice something. Dr. Hypatia's body language is changing. She is leaning forward with more intent, her shoulders now straight; earlier, they had seemed in retreat. Her legs, now uncrossed, are pointed straight ahead. Her eyes are lit up with genuine curiosity.

"I walked down to the park and was exhausted from the events of the day. I fell asleep on a park bench. I awoke to Cam standing over me and laughing at me."

"How did he know you were in the park?" Dr. Hypatia interrupts.

"It's where we normally meet up, I guess." I notice something even more interesting than Hypatia's body language. Each time Cam's location comes up, she inquires more—she seems to do this without fail.

"After that we searched for food. We searched for about an hour. Mainly digging food out of garbage cans and eating whatever we could find. All the anxiety from the day really made me lose my appetite, so I just let Cam eat it all. After that, Cam mentioned that tonight probably wouldn't be the best night to sleep in the shelter because of the events earlier that day. So we were going to go sleep at The Split, but Cam had this idea that we climb up onto a roof in the downtown area and sleep under the stars—away from the danger of the streets. It was a pretty warm Monday night, so I figured it would be nice."

"That's nice," Dr. Hypatia says, forcing out a brief smile.

"Anyway, there is an old abandoned building in Chinatown that was pretty easily accessible, so we pushed a Dumpster underneath it and worked our way up the building. We finally worked our way up to the roof, and it was . . . " I pause.

Dr. Hypatia tilts her head to the side. "It was what?"

"It was so peaceful. The color of the city lights, the lack of noise from the cars below, the gleam of the stars. It all just felt right." I smile briefly as I look at the floor. "I put my bag against the side of the roof and watched as Cam passed out on the far side. We were both exhausted. It took a lot of effort to get up on that roof." I swallow deeply and can feel the uneasiness of my breath as it tries to work its way between my teeth.

"Then what happened?"

"I was an idiot," I say, my tone shallow. "Not only did I lead the man up onto the roof with us by my display at the homeless shelter, I had us trapped."

"Can you explain how you felt?" Dr. Hypatia's pupils seem constricted. *What the . . . this lady is loving this! Every part of my story she seems drawn in more and more. Is this what gives her a thrill?*

The pit in my throat is there again, and I swallow hard. "I . . . I felt like I was on an island out in the middle of the sea, trapped by my own actions. And that wasn't the worst part; I got Cam hurt too. The next thing I remember is the sensation of cold, sharp metal being pressed against my cheek."

There is no more emotion in my voice. The room is silent. No longer can I feel my heart beat or the pulse from underneath my chin. No, the only sound in the room is the quiet ticking of the watch on Dr. Hypatia's left wrist. I look at the ground in an indifferent stupor.

"He said to me, 'Don't make a move and don't try to escape and you won't get hurt.' I remember looking over toward Cam and seeing his lifeless body on the ground. It was at that moment that I truly felt alone. The kind of alone I haven't felt since that . . . night." A tear shows up on the underside of my right eye. It seems to just sit there, neither growing nor falling.

A tempting urge rises within me—to cry. But . . . nothing. Really, all I feel is indifference.

"I elbowed the man in the face the moment he looked away. He got knocked to the side and I darted for the opposite side of the roof, the side with the fire escape. I reached for the fire escape to jump over and I remember feeling the thrill of almost being free. But just as I cleared the concrete wall, I was ripped back onto the roof. I remember feeling scared and worried and . . . alone. Like if I was screaming in a crowd of people and no one could me hear me."

Dr. Hypatia's body language has completely changed. Earlier, she seemed distant. Now she is completely leaning forward, almost covering the Dictaphone on the table.

"As I fell back to the ground, the man pinned himself on top of me, and I remember hearing the sound of the knife smoothly making its way through my flesh. Blood flowed into my mouth and seeped down my chin. I looked up and the man hit me hard in the face. That's the last thing I remember."

Beep! Beep! Beep! A sound rings out in the room. It echoes around the walls.

"Oh my. I didn't realize it had gotten so late," Hypatia says as she frantically presses various buttons on her watch to try and halt the source of the beeps. "That will be all today, Sam. Tomorrow when I come back, I want to hear the rest of the story." Dr. Hypatia rises to her feet and hits the stop button on the Dictaphone. The door to the room opens wide. The two officers outside are waiting.

"Do you need any help, Dr. Hypatia?" one of them says.

"No thank you," she answers, coolly.

She collects all her folders and the Dictaphone, rises to her feet, and starts walking toward the door.

"Sam?" Dr. Hypatia says, slowing, now turning back, before she reaches the door. "Is there anything else you can think of to describe Cam?" She turns her head and looks straight in my direction.

"Not that I can think of," I say quietly. "Just, if you can find record of him, can you reach the shelter and have them tell him I'm alright?"

Hypatia says nothing and quickly turns back toward the door.

"Ma'am," I say as she reaches the door threshold. The chains from my cuffs clank loudly against the table.

Dr. Hypatia's footsteps echo in the hall as they slowly move farther away. The two officers step into the room and walk toward me. I stand up and stare—blankly—at the mirror on the opposite side of the room.

TWENTY

CRACKED MIRROR

The lights just hum as I stare at the reflection from the Room 4 mirror. Nothing exciting, just the infrequent flickering of the lights—the pale contrast of the white walls and the reflection of the light off the metal table. I move my arms up and down the dented surface of the metal table. My cuffs slowly drag across the table. I stare at the lights above until individual pockets of blue creep into my eyes. I blink slowly. The pockets of blue diminish and my normal vision is restored.

The doorknob begins to turn and I hear voices approaching. A high-pitched voice follows a low baritone bellow. The door opens slowly. Then I hear an almost subtle laugh. "Anything for you, Dr. Hypatia. Just let us know if you need anything." An officer stands at the door entrance, showing off a big smile for the approaching doctor. His brow raises and his forehead wrinkles into the underside of his officer cap.

"Today will be a very interesting day," Dr. Hypatia says in a quiet voice to the officer—though I can hear her. "Just please remain alert. I am not sure how he is going to take this news."

What news? What is she talking about?

My heart swells as I feel it lowering itself into my stomach. Every part of me shudders as I probe for what she could possibly be talking about. *What news? Is Cam dead? He can't be—there is no way. No one would even try. I don't know if anyone even could . . . or maybe it's something else. Maybe it is something about my old man? Maybe some money? Maybe some personal belongings left behind.*

Dr. Hypatia's heels click against the floor as she enters the room. She looks up from her files. She lets out a beaming white smile. "Good morning, Sam. How are you today?"

I rustle my chains against the table's surface. Grimacing, I slowly look up at her. "I guess I could be better."

Dr. Hypatia has little expression as she sets her large folders on the desk. She slowly pulls out her chair and glances at her watch.

"Is there something you would like to tell me?" I ask, confused.

Hypatia continues sorting through her things, casually licking her fingers. Carefully, she pulls out a large blue file. I can clearly read the white label in the middle: "Samuel Case."

"We will get to that," she says, opening the file. She pulls out three documents. Each has a small yellow flag or flags protruding from it. "So," she says as she looks up from the stack of papers, her tone now quite serious. "For the sake of time, we are just going to jump in today."

She pulls out the Dictaphone and places it face up. She presses the red button and returns to positioning her files. They seem to be perfectly laid out before her, with even three-inch gaps between them.

"This is Dr. Hypatia with Samuel Case. For the record, Sam, I want to make clear my intentions before we begin. Is that OK with you?" She looks toward me and waves her hand for me to speak.

I nod.

"A response please, Mr. Case," she says, her tone firm.

I feel the pit in my throat again work down toward my stomach. "Umm, I agree to whatever it is you want me to do."

"Excellent," she says, a small smile on her face. "It is my professional job as a forensic psychologist to evaluate people in all psychological fields designated by the state and for their own defense. This means, for lack of a better term, that it is my duty to evaluate a person and deem whether they are 'fit.' Meaning, the person understands the criminality of their actions, or I aid in their rehabilitation until the person has reached a certain point of competency.

"As such, are you ready to begin our session?"

"Yes, ma'am," I say quietly. I retreat back into my chair; I can hear the chains rattle with me as I move.

"Alright. When we left off yesterday, you were on top of the roof, and the last thing you remember is looking up from the ground after your lip and cheek had been cut in half and Mr. Savage had knocked you out. Correct?"

"Yes, ma'am," I answer. The nerves in my face seem to tingle. Every thought, every idea, every image from that night makes the hair on my arms seem to stand up. My breath seems shallow.

"Alright. Well, prior to these events occurring, you spoke of a man named Cam, or sometimes he is called Cameron. Correct?"

"Just Cam, ma'am."

"My apologies. Just Cam." She seems to quickly make a few notes. "Just one moment," she says as she stares again at her notes. Then she removes her glasses and looks up at me. She pushes a file in my direction. "Go ahead. Take a look." Her voice seems to rise, maybe even screech. *Is she nervous about something?* I look at her to get a closer read. Her cheeks are flush. The bags under her eyes look heavy. The upper left side of her lip twitches just a bit.

I extend my hand across the table. With each inch, the cuffs scrape against the metal below. I pull the folder closer into my body. The label reads: "Samuel Case -- Medical File."

I open the file carefully. A picture of me in a hospital gown dominates the upper portion of the page. I am heavily sedated. My arms hang over the hospital bed. My right cheek is heavily bandaged with gauze applied on each side of the wound. Several monitors are connected to my body. An IV is taped to my left arm. A finger monitor sits on the end of my right index finger. Several bruises outline my face.

"What do you want me to do with this?"

She points at the page. "As I'm sure you can see from the label on the front of your file, this is the medical report from when you visited the hospital last week."

I look through the various pages and glance across the words: *A large laceration runs from the lateral spect of the mouth, perforating the buccal mucosa, and stopping just shy of the mandibular ligaments.* Complex medical jargon like this fills the pages as each sentence goes on to describe the intricacies of the cut, or "laceration," as doctors call it.

I scan the rest of the pages—blood work, urinanlysis—an endless list of numbers. The list of workups and charts goes on for about forty pages.

I look up. "I don't exactly understand what you want me to take away from this. Isaac Adler told me when I was meeting with him that my toxicology report after the scene of the crime was 'free of foreign substances.'" I motion with my fingers to make quotations for those last four words.

"That is true. Your toxicology report did show no foreign substances in your bloodstream at the time of the murder." Dr. Hypatia is no longer looking at me but again staring down at her notes.

"So . . . what do you want me to take away from this huge medical file? What? I have problems, and doctors want to make themselves feel better by throwing in a ton of verbose words?"

She shakes her head. "No, not at all. But please turn to page 17 of the file."

I rapidly turn pages and arrive at 17. This was the page in this file with the yellow flag. *Wow, I feel like a moron. I could have guessed she wanted me to turn to the page that was marked.*

"Neurotransmitter Assessment and Balance Test," I say as I try to work my way through the words. I scan farther down the page. *Dopamine: High, Serotonin: Imbalance, GABA: Imbalance, Norepinephrine: Regulatory Levels.* I place the file back on the table and look up. "I don't understand what you want me to take away from this."

"I will get to that in a minute," she says as she reaches for the file and pulls it toward herself. "Neurotransmitter assessment tests are infrequently used for someone making a random ER visit. The ER doctor who was on call the night or day that you arrived ordered one due to the abnormality of your injuries. He figured the wounds may be self-inflicted—or, that they could have resulted from a mental illness. Following procedure, he requested a neurotransmitter workup.

When the levels came back as irregular, a full workup was requested."

"You think I inflicted these wounds on myself?"

"I am not sure," she quickly responds. "Or at least the toxicology report would show evidence of a foreign substance such as methamphetamine usage or another drug if one believed the injury to be the result of drug-induced self-harm."

"OK, so I come back to my question, then. What's the point of all this?" I am getting more aggravated. "Just get to the point already! I am sick of dancing around the question."

Hypatia closes the file. She pushes it neatly to the left, just out of my reach. She realigns it with the rest of the folders in her neat little line.

"Dr. Hypatia, if you would be so kind to answer my question, please."

She reaches for another file and pushes it in my direction. I extend my arm slowly and reorient the file so I can read it. It's clear: "East Hills Shelter Residence Files." I flip the file upright and peer down at the numerous pages. This time, instead of one flagged page, there are two.

I flip the file back and open it up to the first page. *Residence Number 11734 – Samuel Case. Registered Visit Dates: 3/12, 3/15, 3/21, 4/10, 4/17 . . .* The list goes on until the final date: *9/3.*

I look up at Dr. Hypatia. "These are all just dates that I stayed at the homeless shelter overnight. If you are trying to make a point, can you please just get on with it?" All I feel is aggravation, and it comes out in my tone.

"In a moment." Her voice is firm. "I believe it will be more prudent for you to come to this realization for yourself. Now, please flip to the second marked page."

I quickly flip the pages until the second yellow flagged page lays in front of me: "Alphabetically Ordered List of Residents." I scan down the page to find a name highlighted in yellow: *Samuel Case – Male – Age: 18.* Adjacent to my highlighted name is, again, the list of days I visited the shelter.

"Alright, sweet," I say. "It's my name again. Awesome." I clench my fists and blow out a big exhale. I look toward Hypatia. She stares back at me with a blank face—nodding slowly, subtly—urging me to look more closely at the page.

"Do you see an alphabetical listing for someone named Cam on there, or Cameron?"

I scroll through the page as I trace my finger downward.

"Yeah. There is a guy here named Cameron Daws. That is probably him. Wow, Daws is his last name. That's kind of lame," I giggle as I look at Dr. Hypatia. Her face remains stoic, as if she is displeased with me laughing. I shrug.

She shakes her head slowly. "I thought maybe this was the man you mentioned so much yesterday. I called the shelter and asked them to describe the man in detail, or to send over a picture if possible. The woman at the front desk and the people in the back office said they had no pictures of Cameron Daws. But what they lacked in an image, they made up for in description. I cross-checked your description of Cam with the description of Cameron Daws, and there is no match. Cameron Daws is a white male, around five-foot-eight. He is about 29 years old—scruffy, dislikes bathing, and is partly Latino in ethnic- ity. The man you described to me is a 42-year-old war veteran who is black and cleanly shaven—as of now—but before, you said, he had a large scruffy beard.

"OK," I say, confused. "Then he is probably the next one on the list." I redirect my eyes to the page, to where my finger is resting. Above Cameron Daws is a name, Bradley Tomb. And below that name is someone named Chris Perkins. I look up, confused.

"I still don't understand. Where is Cam's name? Shouldn't he be here, somewhere?"

Dr. Hypatia's face is now very still; there is no facial motion at all. She motions for me to continue looking at the page. "Do you see a man on there with the name Cam or Cameron anywhere, other than Cameron Daws?"

I whip my eyes up and down the list. Rapidly, furiously looking . . . *Jason Barrett . . . no. Desean Brown . . . no. Chris Comer . . . no, no, no!*

I quickly push the file away. "He's not there! Why isn't he on that list? Did the homeless shelter staff just forget about him and decide they didn't want to include him?"

"Can I have that file back for a moment?" Dr. Hypatia asks.

"I . . . umm . . . I don't understand. What's going on? Why isn't Cam listed here? Where is he? Where's Cam?" My voice gets more shrill with each question. I can feel a chill down the back of my spine.

Dr. Hypatia reaches for the folder and begins to pull it to herself. I slam my hand on the folder. The clanking of the chains is loud. "You're not getting this file back until I get some answers!" I scream.

"Very well," says Dr. Hypatia, giving me a small nod. She now slides a final folder, a blue one, over to me. She sits back in her chair and crosses her arms and legs. My hand is shaking as I reach for the folder. I slowly lower my hand onto the file and pull it to myself. The pit in my throat is getting deeper; I try to push it down. I pull the folder just beneath my eyes. I'm now glaring at the file. It reads "Carrington Boarding School," and it has the school logo. Just under it: "Samuel Case." I swallow at the thought of opening the file. Shaky, I remove a leather band so I can open it.

The first page reads the same as the front. A yellow flag protrudes from near the top of the file folder. I move my fingers slowly up to the top of that page and pull it open. The page falls into my left hand as I read the page title: *Behavioral Characterization: Samuel Case.* My eyes fall to the bottom of the page as the words slowly unfold before my eyes.

Samuel Case is an extremely intelligent young man. Consistently, Sam completes all of his homework and performs in the 99% of his class-mates. He is currently in line to receive the salutatorian award pending continued academic excellence at the end of the year. Just below an academic evaluation area lies another subsection: *Social Behavior.* My eyes work their way down to the subsection box. *Sam Case has endured severe traumatic events within the last year of his life. Because of these events, he has become extremely anti-social, removing himself from any group activities and socializing within various peer groups. When placed in such situations, anxiety attacks are often a common occurrence and he must be immediately removed—so as to avoid harm to the other students.* Just below the subsection is an italicized note: *Aggressive toward people who touch or talk about the scar on his right forearm. When asked about the origin of the scar, Sam tends to react in a violent manner.*

I look up. "So why tell me this? Why show me any of this? I don't understand what you are conveying to me!"

Dr. Hypatia picks up her dark glasses and carefully places them on the bridge of her nose. She cups her hands together and leans forward. "Sam, when I called the homeless shelter yesterday to compare the notes you had given me, something didn't quite add up. The description of the man you gave, the one who accompanied you throughout these past few months . . . Sam, he doesn't exist. Well, let me say this first: at least in the sense of a paper/digital trail.

"But as far as I am concerned, he's not real from an evaluative standpoint."

Dr. Hypatia lets out a heavy sigh. With each breath, the anger swells in my stomach. My skin feels hot, pressed. It's almost as if each individual hair on my arm is standing up. She presses her glasses against her face one more time.

"No, that's not possible! I see him! I *saw* him! He is real! He has been with me every step of the way! There is no way he is not real! I fucking see him all the time! What right do you have to say someone isn't real? You don't even know him!" In one motion, I slam my feet against the floor. With all the force in my upper body, I yank upward—banging the chains against the metal clamp holding them in place.

I can't stop. "What the fuck would you know? Just because he isn't in some document somewhere doesn't mean that he isn't real!" My voice screams out in a mix of emotions: rage, anger, despair, grief, denial. Each squeal of my voice gets higher . . . higher. Each second, a heart-wrenching pounding inside my chest.

Dr. Hypatia remains calm, and she continues to look directly at me.

"Sam, let me ask you something."

I lift my head in her direction. My face feels awkward; I feel dismay—as though I don't know the correct emotion to display. I feel anger—it swells in my stomach. I feel despair—it swells in my heart. I feel lost—it shakes itself in my hands. Finally, I feel alone—it looms over my body.

"Sam?" Dr. Hypatia asks, her voice now quiet.

Tears swell as I concentrate with everything I have to hold them in.

"Sam, do you see Cam right now? Is he in the room with us right now?"

I slowly turn my head and look at both sides of the room. There is no one in the room except for the two of us. The hum of the lights above otherwise permeates the silence. I look side to side—unsure what I am looking for.

"Why would he be *here*?" I ask. Tears start falling down my face. "I don't understand you."

"What don't you understand?" Dr. Hypatia says, leaning against the table.

"I don't understand why you want to take the one thing in my life that I have left. I had absolutely everything. I had a mom. I had a dad. I had a warm room that was safe and comfortable. All it took was one night, and then a ripple effect, to ruin my whole, entire life. Everything was taken from me. My mom, that jackass of a father, my house, my identity. And do you know what then became the one stabilizing factor in my entire life?"

Dr. Hypatia shakes her head, slowly.

"It was Cam!" I cry out. "He was the one person who convinced me to keep going. To leave all of these demons behind. To push past them and become something greater than I ever was—to become stronger. Cam! And then you tell me that he isn't here. So, yeah, I will humor you. I will look around the room one more time for my best friend in the world, who I am sure is sitting out in the city right now contemplating how he can ever possibly see me again." I whip my head around the room, back and forth, scanning every possible corner, crevice, shadow.

Nothing.

"I can tell you with certainty that there is absolutely no one in this room besides the two of us. But Cam is real. He's outside these walls right now, probably panhandling for money." I pause and think. "Well, actually, probably not. Because he sucks at bringing in money." A smile creeps out of my anguish and, for a moment, overtakes my face.

"Are you sure?"

I scan the room one more time. *Yes, sure. No Cam.*

A weight lowers itself onto my shoulder. *No . . .* My heart seems to collapse into the lower part of my abdomen. The room holds still. I look toward Dr. Hypatia. The look on her face is the same as it has been for some time now—stoic, blank. I slowly close my eyes. Tears surface again and slowly creep down the side of my nose and rest above my lips. I lower my head onto the table and slam my hands against it.

Dr. Hypatia says nothing. The room is once again in silence following the reverberations of the chains against metal.

"No! No! You can't be here! It's not physically possible!" I scream. As the words fall from my mouth, a garbled tone accompanies them. "It's just not possible!" I slam my head into my hands on the table. "It's just not possible!" Tears, and now snot, are running down my face. Each breath seems more difficult to take.

"Sam . . . *is he here?*" Dr. Hypatia asks again, quietly. She reaches over to try and touch my hands, extended, on the table. Upon touch, I quickly retract them into my body. My insides hurt. It feels as though everything is going into self-destruct. My abdomen is on fire. My heart won't stop pounding.

I lift my head from the table. *Maybe they made it up. Maybe it's some kind of psychology trick to make me think that I am crazy . . .*

But then it happens: I slowly turn my head and Cam walks into view. *No . . .*

He is different. His face is cleanly shaven and his head is completely bald. He is wearing a white jumpsuit with an ID number stitched into the right pectoral area. Cam walks to the other side of the room, his back turned, and slowly places his hand against the mirror. I look at the mirror. There is no reflection of Cam! No large black man placing his hand against the mirror, only the emptiness of the room.

My eyes fill with tears as I lower my head into my hands. "No, no, not you too! You were the only one left! You were the only one left! *I trusted you!* How could you not tell me? Huh? Tell me! How could you not tell me!" I swing my hips back, launching the chair I'm sitting on into the air.

A loud bang hits the door. "Dr. Hypatia? Is everything alright?"

She turns her head toward the door, but not her body. "Everything is fine. Please, don't come in!"

I turn to face Cam, who has stepped away from the mirror. "You are the only thing I have left! There is no way you can be here right now. You should be outside! Running around downtown looking for McChickens or something."

All I can hear in the background is the sound of Dr. Hypatia reaching for the Dictaphone and shoving it slowly, gently toward me. I lift my head from the cradle of my hands and peer in her direction—and then directly behind her at Cam. Realizing I am no longer looking at her but now looking at someone else, she turns her body to look at the mirror behind her.

Cam slowly makes his way back toward the mirror. With one hand placed against it and his body turned toward me, he stoically stares directly in my eyes. Finally, I hear him speak.

"Sam. Do you remember when we were at The Split the other day and I said, 'I hope for your sake and my own that you never figure out the other aspect of homelessness'?"

I nod; I do remember. I press my hands against my head as it rings out in pain. Tears are now pouring down my face. Dr. Hypatia looks back and forth between me and the mirror. She repositions her chair. She wants to be able to fully watch this interaction.

"Yes, I remember. I remember exactly what you said," I mutter. "To be honest, I don't think I will ever forget it. But I didn't truly understand what you meant."

"What exactly did I say?" Cam asks. He is staring at me intently.

"You said that there are two aspects of homelessness. There is the side of freedom where, out here—or more so out there, in the world—we are free. We could do as we pleased with no rules defined and constructed by 'them.'"

Cam nods, agreeing. "Yes, you are right. But what do you think I mean by 'them'?"

The tears are coming in a torrent now, but I press on. "By 'them,' you mean her." I motion with my finger toward Dr. Hypatia as she continues looking back and forth. *Is she seeing exactly what she thought she'd see? Is she flabbergasted by all this—or expecting it?*

"Yes, but what was the second part? The most important part?"

I push my hands to my face to try and wipe away the newest tears working their way down. "You said there was another part. The part of homelessness where we are misunderstood and shackled. The part where we are silenced. The part where we are confined."

Cam nods again. "Do you understand now what I was trying to tell you? I need you to understand what I mean."

My stomach burns and my heart pounds against the insides of my chest. I clutch my white jumpsuit and collapse on the table. But then I slowly pick it up and nod in response. "Why would you not tell me?" I scream in a garbled mess of tears.

Cam smiles briefly and then relaxes his face. "I didn't know."

"What do you mean you didn't know? You didn't know that you weren't real?!"

Cam nods as he returns to a smile and then closes his eyes. "I didn't know I wasn't real—because you believed I was real."

"So, when I was on that roof and I peered over and you were lying there in a dead stupor . . . that wasn't real? Or how about when I woke up and you were no longer on the roof with me? Or when we were at the shelter, all those times, and you were nowhere to be found? Or at the boarding school, when you would speak to me outside the fence? Or when we . . . " I collapse in heavy tears, feeling my heart banging on the inside of my ribs, as though trying to get out. My arms pulse with shock.

"Sam?" says Cam as he walks away from the mirror and to the right side of the table. "You couldn't take the strain of what was happening to you. All those demons that you held onto. The death of your mother by your father's hand, the one who had to find your father hanging from the ceiling banister by suicide, the rape that awful man exposed you to, everything you have been through." Cam's voice is rising as he goes on. "Everything that you have been through was killing you. You needed a way to cope. A way to survive. So I was incepted. On some level, subconsciously, you knew I wasn't real. You knew . . . that you were on the crux of a breaking point."

Cam breathes in deeply and then shrugs. He places his hands on the table and lets out another heavy sigh. "When you agreed to leave the boarding school and come out onto the streets, something within you changed. I could feel it. You were happy. The demons of your past no longer haunted you. You were finally free to be normal—away from what society expected of you. I am not saying that homelessness is always the answer, but for you, this was your sanctuary—away from them." He points at Dr. Hypatia, and I look back and forth between his finger and her.

Dr. Hypatia is watching me, notepad in hand. She frantically jots down notes and stares back up at me every few seconds.

The tears stop falling as I wash away the last of them with a swift swipe of my hand.

"So, let me ask you something, then," I say to Cam.

"Sure," he says, flashing a smile.

"What now?" I ask.

"Now? Now you are going to experience the other side of insanity, as defined by *her*." Cam points at Dr. Hypatia. "I will be with you until the end, or at least until they silence me chemically. Anything that you need, I will always be there for you."

Cam presses himself off the table and walks back toward the one-way mirror. He slowly turns his head back. He smiles at me as he places his hand against the mirror. Starting from a top diagonal position of the mirror, a crack rings out into the room; a divide in the mirror slowly works its way down to where Cam's hand is positioned. As it reaches his hand, it slows.

"This is your reality now, Sam. This is the reality that you chose." The split in the mirror passes through the underside of his hand and continues down to the bottom right side of the mirror. Cam removes his hand from the mirror and turns his body, positioning himself to face me directly.

I look up and just stare. He's grinning from cheek to cheek.

"Sam?" Dr. Hypatia asks as I turn my attention back toward her, quickly. Now I swivel back toward Cam. But . . . *he's gone . . .*

The crack splitting the mirror from the upper left corner down to the lower right corner has disappeared. The hum of the lights once again fills the silence in the room.

I look back toward Dr. Hypatia.

"What now?"

EPILOGUE

My goal in writing this book is to change the current paradigm of homelessness. The strife, hazards, and nebulousness of everyday life these people encounter is daunting. Consistently searching for a meal, seeking out shelter for the dangerous nights, and the overwhelming task of seeking out health care are all obstacles for the homeless. Throughout *Us People,* I refrained from calling the homeless, *homeless*. My goal in this was to provide Cam a frame of context for Sam. Without a label, Cam was able to show Sam that there is much more to homelessness; human emotions that characterizes us all, regardless of setting and environment. The manifestation of Cam from Sam's co-consciousness represents a massive aspect of the homeless landscape—mental illness. A study conducted by the National Institute of Mental Health in 2009 found that the incidence of mental illness is as high as 20 to 25 percent in homeless people compared to the national average of 6 percent. Homelessness and mental illness are real issues. My goal in this book is to change the way *all of us* think about homelessness. If you can, I urge you to reach out to your local homeless shelter and volunteer! Anything helps, and shelters are always looking for more volunteers.

For more information, please visit:
http://www.nationalhomeless.org